LOVE KILLS

ISMITA TANDON is 'A Lesser Known Poet'. Her poem 'I Am Beautiful' won a prize in the Yahoo-Dove Indibloggers contest. She's also the author of the romantic thriller *Love on the Rocks* (2011) and the crime thriller *Jacob Hills*.

Ismita went to Sophia College, Ajmer, where she studied Economics, History and Sociology. After acquiring an MBA and doing a brief stint in the foreign exchange division of Thomas Cook, Mumbai, she took up poetry and prose wholeheartedly.

She's currently working on *The Song of the Sufi Masroof*, a book of photographs and poems. Ismita blogs at www.lesserknownpoet.com.

LOVE KILLS

Ismita Tandon

HarperCollins *Publishers* India

First published in India in 2014 by
HarperCollins *Publishers* India

Building 10, Tower A, 4th Floor, DLF Cyber City, Phase II,
Gurugram Haryana – 122002, India
www.harpercollins.co.in

ISBN: 978-93-5029-835-0

2 4 6 8 10 9 7 5 3 1

Typeset in 11/14 Californian FB at
SURYA

Printed and bound at
MicroPrints India, New Delhi

To Papa with Love

Will you not take me with you
When you leave?
Said the little girl to her father.
Do they not laugh in heaven, kiss or cry?
A man can surely
Come visit his family once in a while.
Can I at least write to you, if I miss you?
And that I will.

The proud nose turned red
From shame.
He had taken the easy way out.
The body was dying, the spirit lived.
The funeral was not until tomorrow,
They whispered.

Prologue

Watching him die was not all that unpleasant. Only, the smell of burnt meat lingered long after the flames had been doused. The officers carried away the charred remains of my father hurriedly, and the crime scene was cordoned off to keep nosy neighbours and concerned relatives from messing up the evidence.

No one paid attention to me as I slid under the barricade tape and headed to my father's study, which was directly across the living room, where father in his inebriated state had burnt himself to death. And then, the circus at midnight: flashing sirens, indiscreet walkie-talkies and groggy policemen.

Fortunately, the mahogany desk had not suffered much damage except the loss of a carved leg and its glossy varnish. The files on the desk had not been so lucky. Good for me, I thought. Who would want to go through tiresome files only to discover a mountain of debt?

I tried the bottom drawer; it was jammed. I pulled harder and the knob came off. Hell! The envelope had been in for the last six months and I had never bothered with it. The envelope was of no use, obviously, while Father was alive and hitting the bottle.

Even as a child, I knew that this was not how other people thought. It was a little alarming at first, but over the years, I have come to be quite comfortable with my cunning. The Centre of Advanced Mental Abilities (CAMA) in Ooty has a diagnosis for my 'condition': a high IQ. Mom first took me to them when I was six and my teachers refused to let me sit in the classroom. They complained they spent more time trying to answer my questions than teaching. The questions were almost always intelligent and they were often unable to answer them.

A series of tests later, I was declared a gifted child with an IQ of 150. The people at CAMA, however, were disappointed as I showed no inclination towards building a computer or a circuit, or undertaking any kind of scientific mathematical activity. It took them almost three years to realize that it was the study of the human mind that fascinated me. That was about the time Mom died of a broken heart.

Anyway, huddled near the drawer, I looked for the silver-framed photograph of Mom that stood on it. The photo and the frame had miraculously survived the fire – I felt like it was beckoning me to pull at the drawer once again. I stuck the knob back in and tugged at the drawer again. This time, it worked. Mom always took my side, no matter what mischief I'd been up to. Still smiling at the memory of her, I slit the envelope open.

'Don't touch anything.'

The voice belonged to a policeman who had rookie written all over him. From his neatly combed hair to his crisp, newly stitched uniform, he appeared to have stepped right out of the police training academy into our living room.

'I live here and that is . . . was my father.'

'His body isn't even cold yet and you are going through his things?'

'My behaviour must appear odd to you, the lack of tears and general remorse, etc. But I suffer from a rare condition that doesn't allow me to be demonstrative.'

'What condition?'

'Dry tearducts.'

'Huh, what's in your hand?'

'My inheritance.'

'Quite the grieving son.'

'I've got bigger things to worry about.'

'Name one.'

'Bankruptcy.'

'If there's nothing in that will for you, why are you still smiling like the cat that got the cream?'

'Father's bankrupt alright, but mother's money comes to me, now that he's dead.'

'Enough to want your father dead?'

'Plenty! But I didn't kill him, even though he wasn't very likeable most part of the day.'

The officer glared at me.

'I'll get going, Officer, need to see the arrangements.'

'What's the rush? Banks don't open till morning.'

'I was thinking more on the lines of the funeral arrangements.'

'We'll need your statement. I hope for your sake, you have an alibi.'

'Iron-clad, Officer.'

'I'll keep that for now.' The envelope was out of my hand before I knew it and a look of puzzlement crossed the young officer's face as he read its contents.

'This leaves everything to Johnny W.'

'I know.'

'He named you that?' he asked, thumb pointing over his back to where the stretcher carrying my father's roasted corpse lay just minutes ago.

'A die-hard Johnny Walker fan, if ever there was one.'

'Being named after a brand of whisky never bothered you? Seems like a good enough reason to bump your father off.'

'I actually quite like my name, and it's Will not Walker, officer.'

'Johnny Will, I see you prefer to use your mother's maiden name. Then again, what's in a name?'

'Everything. Maybe Shakespeare in all his wisdom didn't know it then, but I do.'

'So young and so wise.'

'Yatha naam tatha gun, in our name lies our talent, our destiny.'

'What are you planning to do, Johnny boy, open up a distillery with all the money Daddy left you?'

'Why wait years to watch people die.'

'Torching them is faster you mean?'

'I am an ordinary kid. Try convincing a judge that I committed this crime to get the money that is already mine.'

'All the law needs is proof, fat boy.'

'Go find some!' I pointed to a white sheet on the floor, which had a sketch of my father's last moments in agony.

He quickly bent down to pick up the paper and took in the caricature of my father screaming for help while the flames enveloped his body. His bony arms raised in horror trying to douse the flames from his body. Terror-filled eyes gazing on helplessly. It was grotesque. The officer thought so too, for he left the room convinced beyond doubt that I had killed my father.

That was a mistake my cocky fifteen-year-old self had made – one that came back to haunt me later in life. Two things followed the future I chose for myself: the shadow of my father's death, and the festering animosity of an officer of the law. Both proved fatal.

Thy Will

A master's degree in psychiatry and a high IQ is a lethal combo, one that might corrupt Mother Teresa. My intentions are good, methods questionable and counsel much sought after, but I can and have reformed men and women wasted by alcohol. Do I sound like a paradox?

You would too, if you had a mind split into two. One half that was dumb enough to embark on a crusade against drugs and alcohol, and the other astute enough to realize that having scruples did not necessarily mean a life spent in rubber chappals. I make roughly one crore rupees a year and manage to evade the taxman's hook like an eel slithers on snow. To be clear, I wear handmade Italian leather shoes.

Writing didn't come easy, but then anything that made money was fine by me. I had enough malicious gossip stored in my head to cause an earthquake in the lives of the rich, the famous and the not-so-sober, and if someone was willing to pay me big money for it, I was willing to exercise my writing skills for the *Alcohol Weekly*.

I like to write in the confines of my study, the all masculine and oak atmosphere works for me. From my chair, I can see

Adam's Edge, the deep valley filled with mist round the year. There's a dirt road leading to Adam's Edge, and all around the grass has dried, turned stiff, crystallized. It's awfully quiet, chilly too, like the winter afternoons I spent chasing butterflies as a child. From where I sit, the dirt road seems never-ending, but of course it does lead to that plunging valley – a place that holds many memories for me, some quite ugly.

A hundred-year-old house, after all, has many stories to tell. It was built by Great Grandfather Zachary Will in 1890, when the timber business was at its peak. Zachary believed in a merciful God (unlike me; I've got issues with that fellow), and named the colonial structure 'Thy Will'. The influence of French architecture can be seen in the high ceiling and the tall arched windows that keep the house perennially cold. The porch is marble, imported all the way from Italy. It is perhaps the grandest and most beautiful entrance in the whole of Monele.

There are three large bedrooms, a big dining hall, a living room and my study on the ground floor.

The rooms on the first floor have not been aired since my mother passed away twenty years ago. There are antique treasures scattered around the house. I have been approached many a time by art dealers to sift through my heritage and make a neat profit of it, but I don't have the heart to walk through those rooms and revive old, painful memories. All that antique furniture and precious chandeliers – and I am the sole occupant and heir of this imposing mansion.

There have been some changes, though. Six years ago, I set up a rehab facility to help alcoholics and druggies sober up. The outhouse of my bungalow was converted into a modern two-storeyed facility for the rich suckers who wanted to get a fix on their 'little' alcohol problem. The fee was enormous and restricted the entry to men and women rich enough to spend lakhs on imported malts every month. Secrecy was of utmost importance to them and the rehab facility offered the perfect cover to rest and recuperate in the lap of nature. And despite my issues with God, I chose to name the rehab 'Thy Will' after my plush bungalow.

We are much in demand. However, the phenomenal success of the centre has done precious little for my reputation; former patients barely acknowledge my presence if I accidentally run into them on the street and the present ones come with a fixed opinion of me: a crook selling a cure.

The buzz is that I cheat innocent men and women of their lives' savings. The only reason they come to me is that no such facility in the country guarantees recovery from alcohol and/or drug addiction while maintaining complete secrecy.

At the rehab, we follow a long-term treatment model popularly known as Therapeutic Community (TC), a residential treatment for alcohol and drug addicts in a non-hospital setting.

The treatment lasts anywhere from three to six months, and starts with getting rid of the alcohol present in the patient's bloodstream: a process that can only be undertaken by a licensed medical facility, because without the strictest care, it could result in serious physical, psychological and emotional consequences, even death. At the rehab, our in-patients follow a stringent routine of counselling, behavioural therapy, meditative techniques and other stress-busting activities.

Their day begins at six and it's lights out at eight in the evening, a lifestyle that most of these patients could never have imagined for themselves.

'Thy Will' has been a peaceful place despite its crazy inhabitants, until of course, the death sequence began.

I patiently wait for Sera to come in and brief me about the day's appointments. She joins me every morning around ten, dressed in a calf-length skirt and bright tees with weird messages. Yesterday's tee had a woman pulling her hair out, screaming, 'I don't belong here!' Truth is, Sera fits right in like the missing block in a child's puzzle.

An understaffed rehab facility can be a nightmare. I had to advertise for help in the newspaper. Only one applicant seemed more than eager to join and since most applicants weren't willing to live in a place as remote as Monele, Sera came to be the resident psychologist. It's been four long years since she came to live here.

She has a no-nonsense air about her, but gives the word 'tardy' a whole new meaning. According to her, the whole universe conspires to make her late every single day of the calendar year. I think it's an old habit from her upper-class upbringing that she has no intention of kicking.

It is 10.20 a.m. and the wonder girl is still missing. Five more minutes later, she walks in and dumps two parcels on my desk. I just about manage to save the coffee from spilling.

'Why do you have to buy all this from that silly baker every morning? Why don't you ask Marie to bake whatever you want?' I growl.

'Your housekeeper has her hands full. Besides, I happen to like the silly baker. It's a delight to watch his strong hands smooth a hot batch of cookies from the oven.'

'You have been buying stuff from him all these months in the hope that he'll get rid of his wife and piglets to hook up with you?'

'Oh no, I wouldn't dream of breaking up his marriage and dislocating his eight kids.'

'He really has eight of them? You've got a weird taste in men.'

'I've got a slob for a boss – that should tell you something.'

'You don't mean that?'

'No.'

'Good, because I don't mind if patients badmouth me, but I won't have my staff talking to me like that. It's bad for business,' I say gravely.

Monele is nestled on one of the higher peaks, and is accessible only by road. The cracked asphalt starting from Ooty runs right through its steep incline, dividing the town into two uneven halves. The luxury homes and impoverished huts are sloped on either side, giving the town a haphazard, higgledy-piggledy look. Monele's dawdling economy is supported by the traditional timber industry, small coffee plantations and an old distillery.

The distillery has ensured Monele its place on the map. The rum, known locally as 'Rumbrandt', after the famous Dutch painter Rembrandt, was Great Grandpa Will's idea of a joke. It is transported all across the country and though its taste is nothing to write home about, its price has ensured addiction among the local populace.

The men warm chilly evenings by nursing their drinks, while their women work hard in the tourist establishments that pay their bills. The town boasts of another temptation: marijuana, which covers the misty mountains like moss. Between the rum and marijuana, many families in Monele have collapsed. Young widows are often seen beating their chest at the untimely demise of their husbands, while the children stand dry-eyed and even a little glad to see their abusive, good-for-nothing fathers go.

Grandpa Will had also been a victim of alcohol addiction. The downfall of the great Will family had begun with him. The losses in the timber business led him to the bottle. How was he to know that his dependence on alcohol would have far-reaching effects and in time would ruin the life of his daughter, my mother?

Her sallow, pain-filled face flashes before my eyes. Today seems to be a day for reverie.

Sera comes in again to remind me about my afternoon appointment with the general. She does not wait long; her noon group-therapy session awaits her.

I did the right thing, employing a woman against my better judgement. She is not only competent and dedicated, but also has a rare sensitivity that makes patients open up.

Four years ago, when I had gone to pick up Sera from the town bus stop, I remember how she stood by the signboard that read 'Town's Population: 662', surrounded by two giant trunks, a suitcase and two bags, looking like a mail-order bride arriving with her trousseau.

She held one hand on her head to stop the wind from

blowing back her waist-length hair. She wore a thin floral dress, expensive yet understated, and made for her slender figure. I remember thinking, oh boy, I had advertised for a psychologist and got a hot mamma instead. I mouthed a silent prayer, God, please let her brain be as impressive as the rest of her. There was so much to do at Thy Will; I had been putting in twenty hours a day. I needed a day labourer, not a frigging showpiece!

'Doctor Sera, welcome to Monele. I am Johnny Will.'

Her hand was rough and very unlike the rest of her.

'I hope I haven't kept you waiting too long, Doctor Will?'

'Call me Johnny. Everybody does, and it's no sweat waiting for a pretty lady. The only part that baffles me is how am I supposed to fit those trunks in the boot of my car?'

'I am really sorry about that. It's just books and some clothes.'

'Oh.'

'Five years of marriage, one tends to accumulate quite a bit,' she explained.

I remembered reading about her separation in her resume.

'But my real possessions are intangible and can't be put in a box, Doctor Will.'

Her open, matter-of-fact manner was what convinced me that I had found my Man Friday.

My afternoon appointment sits in the large hall outside my office, dishevelled, angry and abusive. I begin to review the progress report of the decorated general. Habitual drinking had led to an error of judgement that had caused the loss of ten civilians and twenty soldiers in insurgency-ridden Kashmir. The incident was swept under the carpet, employing the usual political bullshit about a sudden ambush sprung by a jihadi outfit. The general was just sent home quietly, not court-martialled. He had after all spent thirty-four years serving his country, even if most of them were spent sipping whisky.

A proud man, the guilt and disgrace did him in and the bottle became a constant companion, so much so that his friends didn't visit him any longer and his daughter refused to bring the grandchildren over. He was a bad influence.

Left alone, he would have drank himself to death, but his timid wife put shame aside and sought outside help. She walked into our office three months ago and begged Sera to give her some kind of a concoction that, when mixed in an alcoholic's diet, makes him allergic to alcohol. She had picked up this bizarre information off the back of a taxi, or so she said. Sera had a tough time explaining to this elegant, nervous woman that it took more than just some white powder to break the habit of a lifetime.

On Sera's advice, she brought in her husband the next day for a psychometric test to gauge the deterioration his mind had suffered. While the general sat hunched over the questionnaire, I interviewed Mrs Baines.

'I want you to be completely honest with me because you are a part of the treatment.'

'Alright.'

'How long?'

'I told you yesterday, two years since he retired and took to the bottle.'

I intervened: 'What would you gain from lying to me at

this point, Mrs Baines? Your husband's mind is dying and his body is turning to waste. His cognitive functions are greatly compromised; even a fool can see that he has been at it for years. Why didn't you seek help before?'

'People . . . our relatives and children thought that, being a decorated soldier, he would have the willpower to give it up. Why wash our dirty linen in public?'

She spoke with utmost dignity, the ravages of time and alcohol had not dimmed her sense of society and social stigma.

I wondered then whether she too was to blame – this silently suffering wife who had witnessed it all, fearing for her husband's reputation.

'He's a chronic alcoholic, you know that, don't you? His medal of honour is not going to save his life.'

'All this is so shameful!'

'So you would rather be the widow of a man laid respectfully to death in his finery than be ostracized by a social circus that cares little for you. Where is the sense in that?'

She nodded; there was nothing to refute the truth. We were on the same side after all.

'Look, Mrs Baines, it's not going to be easy. There will be withdrawal symptoms, acute cravings and possible mental and physical breakdown. But all this is temporary.'

'How temporary?'

Once she was recruited, the task was easy. Mrs Baines was quickly made to sign a form, which meant that I could now admit the general in our psych ward.

Sera showed the general into my office, and both husband and wife sat staring at me. The wife was nervous as she had just committed her husband to a rehab without his knowledge or permission.

The general showed signs of agitation; it was noon and the time for his first drink of the day was fast approaching. Beads of sweat sat on his forehead, despite the cold, and his facial muscles were strained with the effort of keeping his hands and body from trembling. If I didn't know better, I would think he was about to have a seizure.

I could no longer keep him in the dark and slowly informed him that he would be our guest for an indefinite period of time. His profanities belied his social status. The wife now seemed terribly unsure of the decision she had made. Being threatened and abused was not new to her, but the intensity with which he delivered those threats was alarming even to my ears.

'Thirty years of marriage and this is what you do to me, you bitch! Lock me up, so you can live in my house! I'll throw you out on the streets. How dare you make a fool of me in front of this quack?'

He started to drag her out of the room. I pressed the buzzer and two well-built orderlies came in and caught hold of the general by his armpits; he resisted his captors, disgracing himself some more in the process.

'You can't keep me here against my will! You bastard! Let me go!' he said, like a five-year-old throwing a temper tantrum.

His face flushed darkly, and he sat down on the floor, refusing to get up. His pleading eyes sought those of his wife, who sobbed silently. I wanted to walk away from it all. Had I not seen the same helplessness in my father's eyes?

I waited.

He threatened, 'I'll kill myself. I am a soldier. I won't die on a hospital bed.'

'Please, they'll cure you and we can go visit the kids, our grandchildren,' Mrs Baines cajoled, kneeling by his side.

'I promise, Preet, you'll never see my face again if you leave me here . . . I'll hang myself.'

This was the alcohol talking. An alcoholic's biggest fear is not getting his daily fix. The craving is so strong that he would rather die than suffer the withdrawal symptoms. They have told me that their stomach churns as if a knife is being taken through it, repeatedly; tremors, nausea, profuse sweating, render the body incapable of performing any function. The mind in the grip of such frenzy begs for the pain to be numbed, be it through drugs or death. The general knew this and that more would be in store if he were to be locked away.

Suddenly, he lunged at his wife's throat. 'I won't let you leave me and go!'

At this point, I had to use a tranquillizer.

The general was finally admitted to the facility barely 200 yards from my office-cum-residence. He was locked up in a room with white walls, grilled windows and a door that locked only from the outside. What made this morose existence a tad interesting was that his room was next to that of an ageing film star – my most violent patient, a psychopath.

Mrs Baines left a few minutes later, tears streaming down her face. I advised her not to visit her husband for some time. The medication required to detoxify the general's body would practically leave him a vegetable for the next two weeks. Not a pretty sight. But she assured me she had seen much worse in her thirty-five years of married life.

She came in every day for the next three months and watched him through the window grille, as he puked, paced, raged and cried like a child. He sat on the floor naked, beating his tiny paunch, begging for a drop of alcohol, pleading with her to free him one minute and calling her an ungrateful whore the next instant. Not once did Mrs Baines flinch. When his gut-wrenching screams echoed through the empty hallway, she softly cooed to him in Punjabi. It would calm him down for a little while, stop the barrage of abuses. In his sleep, he confessed to several fake encounters, naming young boys barely sixteen or seventeen gunned down in crossfire and later propped as jihadis to appease activists from Amnesty International or the Human Rights Commission. The story that scared me shitless was when he described how cold-bloodedly his men forcibly stuffed cyanide capsules down the throat of terrorists who had surrendered their weapons in the hope of being taken alive. In the middle of the jungle, the soldiers chose to play god. The joint operations were run by a special task force created by the army to fight insurgency in J&K in the 1990s, involving the local police and the Border Security Force (BSF). It was a tacit arrangement based on the fact that there was neither enough space in local prisons to lock up the terrorists, nor would the judiciary be competent enough to sentence them to a timely death. So they shot or poisoned the jihadis in broad daylight and buried their bodies in shallow graves in the valley, leaving no trace that these men ever existed. The general's hoarse cries, though seemingly incoherent, were in reality confidential file numbers and details of strategic operations gone awry. He was a ticking timebomb. It was no surprise that he took to drinking.

Eventually, the general did get better and his hallucinations disappeared. We sent him home loaded with pep talk and a bag full of medication. The chances of relapse were the highest in the first few days and a weekly visit was mandatory.

All seemed to be going well, until today. I took in the general's appearance through the glass partition that allowed me a clear view from my office.

'Afternoon, General. Hope all is well.' I stretched out my hand and offered him a chair.

I could see he didn't want to sit. The expensive recliners in my office diffused the anger patients came in with, and the general seemed to know that.

'Why are you taping me, Johnny?'

'Are you not enjoying your performances? Midday matinee, huh?'

'Why are you doing this? I am in control now, just one drink in the evening, that's all.'

'Really, then how did you end up on the floor in your own vomit in the last video?'

'You bastard, you have been watching them!'

'Regularly. And I must admit, I am not particularly delighted to see you with your pajamas down.'

'You son of a bitch, you can't violate someone's privacy like this!'

'Go ahead and sue me.'

I had him cornered, this was not the same general from three months ago who cared little about what society thought of him. As the hold of alcohol weakens, the self grows stronger and a sense of shame, a sense of right and wrong revives.

'I want those tapes back, Johnny. How much money do you want?'

'Your wife's given me plenty. Your treatment wasn't free, you know that, right?'

'What do you want from me?'

'Quit drinking.'

'And what of the tapes?'

'It's merely therapy, General. You don't really think I am going to use them, do you?'

'You are no better than a petty blackmailer. Is that why the other patients don't like to talk about you? You are using their shame to keep them sober.'

'Super! My master plan unravelled in minutes.'

'You are very smart, aren't you? Someday this smartness is going to do you in.'

I opened the door to my office and lead him out.

'I'll keep that in mind, General. Drop by the next time you are around.'

I dismissed him from my mind and devoted the rest of the afternoon to the more tiresome new applicants, screening their lies, listening to lame excuses for their drinking problem like work pressure, marital discord, sexual dysfunction or plain boredom. Wimps, psychopaths, losers, prigs: these were the kind of people I spent my day with.

At six, Sera peeped in to remind me that I had to attend an event at the Seven Seas at eight.

'I am done for the day. Don't schedule anything for the first half tomorrow. I don't know what time I'll be back.'

'Sure boss, have fun.'

'Come along, if you like. It's an exhibition of contemporary art.'

'Think I'll pass your generous invitation and spend a lovely evening looking at ugly pictures.'

'Define ugly.'

'Well, pictures of round-eyed, emaciated children with pot bellies; women suffering from goitre or some other graphic condition. And also, I don't much care for your girlfriend's taste.'

'You don't like Mira, do you?'

She showed me the back of her tee that read, 'MEaN GuRLs'.

'Wow, that's eloquent!'

No retort was forthcoming. Sera just shut the door and went back to filing applications. Her off-hand attitude was a big turn on. I had to remind myself that I had a fiancée.

Five-foot nothing, Mira had the sexiest and most ambitious mind to have walked this earth, or so I believed, until I slept with her. In bed, she was as accommodating as a woman could be. In the early days of our relationship, I was afraid of hurting her in bed; it's a rare woman who tells you she likes it rough. When she constantly made fun of my gentle lovemaking, I switched from tender to forceful, bordering on violent. Sometimes, while humping her, I would catch a glimpse of myself in the mirror and I didn't like what I saw. I was reminded of my father, grunting like an animal, bending over her, sly and hungry. I had, in my anger, at times taken from her more than she wanted to give, but she would laugh it away and say, 'I can take a good pounding, Johnny.'

Mira wasn't all sex and games. She was two different women: one who would writhe and moan in my arms, hot as a summer night and beg me to take her like a common whore, hard and fast; the other, cold and elusive as the morning dew, whose actual prowess lay in the world of high finance, corporate wheeling and dealing and taxable income.

A great mind in a tiny body – in a moment of fondness, I named her Mighty Mouse: a friend, lover and an accomplished liar.

Mira

Orchids for Miss Mouse

My eyes scan the crowd, searching for the face that quickens my pulse. I spot him the moment he enters the hall, lean as an athlete, not an ounce of extra flesh under his white sports coat, and of course, that fork-shaped scar along the jawline of his devilishly handsome face.

He wears his hair long, fashionably nineties. I specially love the way it falls on his forehead, and the way his impatient fingers comb it back. And then there are his eyes, fiery brown, weaving magic, deep, dark and dangerous.

Apart from his name, Johnny has everything going for him: good looks, money and a successful career. I see him looking for me in the crowd, but I don't want to be found just yet.

I calculate my options, to tell or not to tell. We aren't an ordinary couple; we both have our secrets. For now, I don't want him to know mine, one that would change our lives forever.

'Johnny, sweetie, I am glad you could make it!'

'I had to, haven't seen you in days. What's been keeping you busy?'

'I just closed a deal for one of the steel biggies. Why don't we take the weekend off and hit Pondi?'

'Sure, Mighty Mouse, but only if you promise to wear the bikini I got you from Hawaii last summer.'

'You must be out of your mind. I might as well be naked!'

'Prude!'

'Perv!'

'A prude and a pervert, what a nice team we make.' Johnny smiles.

His smile is so heart-warming, I have second thoughts about ruining our evening. We hang about for another hour, appreciate the photographs, congratulate the artist and say our goodbyes. Back at my place, Johnny and I do what we do best, make love. I often wonder if we'll ever get bored of each other, if we will want to see other people who are better in bed and have bigger brains and higher IQs. On second thought, I doubt it. Johnny's rehab facility makes more profits in a year than most blue-chip companies do in the stock market. My job is to ensure that every tax rebate and legal gambit is employed to make these profits appear non-taxable. With ever-changing tax laws, changing governments and the vigilant IT department, my job gets tougher each day. What Johnny does with all that money is anybody's guess.

My own theory is that he is engaged in some activity bordering on the illegal. It is this thrill of living on the edge that makes my association with Johnny so exciting. There isn't a dull moment – except, lately, the fast life is beginning to get to me. Too much is happening and my planned, organized life seems to be spiralling out of control.

I get out of bed to make us a midnight snack and remember the flowers are still languishing on the settee where I threw them last night. I am about to dump them in the wastebasket when Johnny catches me in the act. Can he read my face, spot the colour of guilt? With Johnny, there is no way of telling.

'Super! These orchids must have cost some sucker a bomb.'

'Just an old client.'

'Some clients you have. Mine would send flowers too, but for my funeral.'

'That's ridiculous, they may not love you, but most of them admire you for the work you do.'

He nods absent-mindedly as he continues to stare at the wretched orchids, as if they could reveal not just the identity of the sender, but everything there is to know about him.

Johnny leaves for home a little after three; he never sleeps anywhere but his own bed. I can never do that, live in a place inhabited by crazies, sociopaths and drunkards. At any given time, there are at least five to six patients staying in Thy Will. Even the thought of them writhing in pain, their bodies craving alcohol, gives me the creeps.

Time for some shut eye, my mind tells my body. Still, I decide to clean up before going to sleep. The first stop is the settee, where the flowers lay unattended.

I have this sudden, savage urge to crush and pull them apart. They seem too full of life, mocking me, teasing me. As I tug at their gloating faces, I discover the sender's note in a bold, black handwriting which I must have missed the first time.

To Mira,
A passion flower.
Sweet to taste,

Silk to feel,
Layer by layer . . . heaven to peel.

Johnny knows! And what Johnny knows he finds a way to use against you.

Journal of an Alcoholic

The urge to drink is so strong today, another lonely evening, and the incessant rain splashing at the windowpanes goading me to help myself. To feel the burning sensation down my throat straight from a bottle, to let loose, to be, most of all, not feel the failure my life has come to be. I am suicidal at this point. I am, I know.

Another argument is to kill.

God-man Will says I have to fight this. Fight these destructive tendencies before they destroy me. He can't help me. That lying son of a bitch!

I found something interesting today about Dr Wacko. Half a dozen cases of malpractice have been registered against him in the last five years; that makes an average of one case a year.

Disgruntled patients have some nasty, nasty things to say; one of them even accused him of molesting her during a three-month-long treatment. The lawsuits are withdrawn sooner than they are filed and are settled almost immediately outside court, making Dr Wacko something of a media celeb.

What kind of a fucking doctor gives interviews, saying his patients are troubled people and sometimes troubled people don't know what they are talking about?

That's not true! I know what I am talking about when I say I hate my doc.

He sits in his glass cabin trying to analyse what goes on in my brain. As if all of us alcoholics can be clubbed together as one, displaying certain predictable characteristics which a few pills can cure over time. Dr Wacko thinks with his big fucking brain and smug manner he can fix the pain that plagues my soul?

Then he is horribly mistaken.

I am not addicted to alcohol. I am addicted to the freedom it gives me from societal norms, the fucking drama! No smartass doctor is going to blackmail me and get away with it.

Zac

Mamma's Boy

'Have you asked him for the money, yet?'

'No, Mother, I haven't.'

'Why not, are you afraid of him?'

'Of course not, Mother!'

'Remember Zac, everything Johnny owns is rightfully mine. That evil boy is clever but clever boys often meet a terrible end.'

'Mother, that's a horrible thing to say!'

'How did I give birth to a retard like you? If you had any brains, we wouldn't be begging Johnny for our own money.'

'Mother, please!'

A thick brow arched in question.

'I . . . uh . . . meant I am trying to finish breakfast.'

'Don't disappoint me, Zac.'

'No, Mother.'

Quickly finishing my breakfast, I get into the car and drive straight to Thy Will. My thoughts are of mother. Life played a cruel joke on twenty-two-year-old Adele Will when she became pregnant with a child whose father's name she was unwilling to divulge.

The elder daughter, Daisy, married to a journalist, inherited the huge bungalow, Thy Will, and the acres of land surrounding it.

Johnny was a year older to me and the apple of Grandpa Will's eye, the legitimate grandson and the sole heir to Thy Will. In time the scandal of my birth slowly faded as did Grandpa Will's health but he still did not make any changes to his will.

Johnny and I played in the fields where Aunty Daisy grew vegetables and tended pretty flowers. She was a woman who could love someone else's children just as much as her own, a remarkable woman, unlike her sister Adele.

My childhood was full of fun and laughter and not one of deprivation as my mother would have me believe. I remember Bugsy, Johnny's favourite rabbit and his best buddy in the field. I was terrified of him, but would put on a brave act and pretend to like the red-eyed bunny in front of Johnny.

Those years are a bittersweet mix of memories. Uncle Robin, Johnny's father, would come home drunk and make a scene as he stumbled through the big house in his blue-checked lungi. In fact, he was the first man I had seen naked, for his lungi never remained around his waist past nine o'clock.

Soon, he stopped going to the local bar for a drink and entertained himself at home. The routine evening drinks, the scenes and the drama slowly sucked the life out of Aunty Daisy.

She was found dead in the bathroom one cold December morning. She had slipped and fallen sometime in the night and broken her back. Uncle Robin slept through all of this, a few metres away.

Life became pretty hellish after that. Johnny was now a

very distant ten-year-old, finding comfort in food, and my mother, the ruling queen of the Will Household.

Uncle Robin drank the whole day long, while Mother ran the house with an iron fist and quelled Johnny's rebellious nature with whatever means she deemed necessary. I hero-worshipped Johnny; though he got fatter and fatter with every passing month, in my eyes he could do no wrong. He was invincible. When I was with him, I felt free of Mother. I learnt to fear her in true earnest only after she killed, skinned and cooked the bunny.

It was an evening like no other. Johnny and I couldn't get enough of the succulent meat mother had cooked that day. The feel and taste of the soft fibrous meat lingers on when I think of the events that followed the enjoyable supper. Mother waited till we had licked the pan dry to tell us that Bugsy's paw had got caught in a barbed wire and they had to kill him to end his misery.

'He was such a meaty rabbit. What a waste to go like that, so I thought why not give him a memorable farewell.'

Johnny did not miss the superior tenor in Mother's voice. His expression changed from shock to anger to disgust, and in minutes he was throwing up right there. Smelly chunks of Bugsy's meat lay at my mother's feet. Mother struck a blow to his cheek. I remained rooted to my chair; I wanted to help but could not utter even a word to save him from her wrath. After all, she had just cooked and fed us the red-eyed, furry rabbit, just like the old wrinkled witch in the storybooks. For me, Mother's reign of terror had begun.

It came as no surprise to me, when a few years later, upon Uncle Robin's death, Johnny threw Mother and me out of the sprawling bungalow after making her a decent settlement to set up her own café.

Café Aspen had been my mother's dream and that Johnny should be the one to fulfil it is another quirk of fate. Yet pittance is all it was to Mother and she tells anybody who cares to listen how her nephew cheated her out of her vast fortune. I have no such illusions. I love Johnny as dearly now as I did as a child. After Johnny set up Thy Will, I quit my job as a manager at the Claridges to run the rehab's administrative division. Mother thinks even a clerk can record and file information at the centre, but she is wrong. This is confidential and privileged information and Johnny trusts me with it.

Apart from a more than generous salary, the job has its perks, like respite from Mother's acid tongue, if only for a few hours.

I park the car and enter the house from the side-door, which leads directly to the main office. This door is used by the staff which basically includes me and Sera and a team of well-trained orderlies.

I like Sera and suspect she's in love with Johnny. I wonder what Mira would have to say if she ever found out.

Johnny met Mira as the result of a rave. An overdose of some fancy illegal blend had rendered her comatose for three days. He cleaned her up and made her as good as new. That was even before Johnny knew the identity of her influential father, the owner of Seven Seas' Resort. Kaizad Kermani is a big man in the small town of Monele. Mira had inherited his eyes and cold manner.

The phone in the main lobby rings and Mira's voice wafts over from the other side. I wonder if it is telepathy.

'Hey, Zac, is Johnny in? He's not answering the home phone.' No greetings, no 'hello, Zac, how are you?'

'He's supposed to be with you.'

'He was, until last night. If he's not home, where is he?'

For once I hear Mira sound disturbed. Good! 'I honestly wouldn't know, Mira. He comes, he goes.'

'Yup!' And she slams the receiver down.

Women always get the better of me. I don't know whether to desire or despise them. Maybe it has something to do with the fact that I live with my mother.

Mother, who refused to put me up for adoption and wore the label of being a fallen woman, a whore. She didn't marry because in those days nobody wanted a ready-made family of two.

I know that under all that harshness there's a heart that wants nothing more from life than to love and be loved in return. Her shrill voice and her crass remarks are a cover-up. But to the world, she is just a greedy old maid.

We have had each other's back for thirty-three long years. I love her, but the poison in her mind is slowly making its way into mine. I am beginning to tire of the sordid arrangement of being a mamma's boy. There are days I wish she would just go away to a place from where there is no returning.

I long to be free.

Blackmail

'Never let shame seal your lips.'

'It's written on the wall outside your office.'

'Yes, Mrs Moorthi.'

'My shame has cost me four miscarriages.'

'Why didn't your husband get you treated for alcohol addiction?'

'My husband's a government servant. He was always too busy. And then there was his reputation to worry about.'

'What made you come to us now?'

'He divorced me last month.'

'We'll put you back on your feet, Ms Moorthi. I hope the government servant has made quite a generous settlement to look after your needs?'

'I can certainly afford your expensive fee, if that is what you mean.'

'Good, we'll get started right away.'

I have no compassion for these self-destructive women on the wrong side of forty, struggling to get a handle on their lives. Four miscarriages! What was she thinking? The whole world wants to raise a family, no matter where their own life is headed. Buy a fancy cradle, tiny clothes, expensive toys, paint the nursery and potty train, it's all fine, but what are they going to teach the kid when their own head is so full of fears and lies? How easy it is to make a baby and then screw up with its head! Passing on the confusion and chaos to the child, till the new seed is infected by the old. A shame indeed.

A moment later, Sera comes in. We start to review the in-patients who are up for discharge.

'The general checked in to pick up his fortnightly medication, Johnny. He's not looking good. I told him you were out. Why did you want me to lie to him?'

'There's nothing more we can do for him. It's his war now.'

'He just seems so angry with life.'

'He'll be alright, Sera. He actually threatened me on his way out. Now, that's a good sign.' I chuckle, remembering the look on the general's face as he delivered his warning.

'Johnny, why are we always facing lawsuits and being threatened by our patients? What do you have on them?'

'A whole lot of dirt.'

'Johnny, it's not ethical to use the personal information in their medical records for any purpose other than treatment.'

'Let's just say it's an extended treatment.'

'But isn't the treatment based on reviving their faith in themselves? The first step to healing is faith. You always say that.'

'For most patients it works that way. But for some, faith wears thin, fear reins them in. You control their fear, you control their addiction.'

'What fears?'

I have never seen this hysterical look on her face. A storm

of doubt and disgust floats in her wide eyes, questioning my loyalty to my work. I decide to be truthful.

'I give a clean chit, the patient goes home. In the first few days, the chances of relapse are extremely high, you know that. A certain case or two, I prefer to monitor a little more closely and request Zac to keep me posted.'

'Posted, how?'

'Zac tapes the patient's activity and shows it to him. It evokes extreme embarrassment and aggression, hence the lawsuits and the generous expletives.'

'Are you telling me Zac creeps into people's houses and tapes them while they are making a fool of themselves drinking?'

'Well, when you put it that way, it does sound rather disgusting.'

'That is humiliating and an absolute violation of a patient's privacy!'

'Well, privacy is no good to them if they are dead.'

'But this borders on blackmail!'

'Oh, come on! It's not like I ask them for money. I just want them to lead normal lives.'

'How very magnanimous of you, Johnny!'

'Hey, remember, I am the good guy here.'

'It's sick to tape your patients in their homes without their knowledge. It's twisted!'

'I don't get any sadistic pleasure out of watching a drunk make a play for the fourteen-year-old maid, or beat his children, or rape his wife in his drunken stupor.'

She calms down and asks in a solemn voice, 'You have all that on tape?'

'Worse,' I reply, equally solemnly.

We are quiet for a while, then she looks up and says in a quiet voice, 'Johnny, it's not right. You are not treating ordinary people here. These people are rich, influential and most of them have more hang-ups than just alcohol. You need to be careful.'

'I am.'

She pauses again and shakes her head. 'I really can't believe it. How do you sleep at night?'

'Very well, you could check if you like.' Now why did I say that?

Sera chews on her bottom lip absent-mindedly for a bit, then asks, 'So these patients live in the constant fear of you leaking their private information?'

'A few do, I guess.'

'Damn, Johnny, I didn't sign up for this. I wanted to help people become better human beings, not blackmail them into doing your bidding.'

She pushes her chair back with force and storms out of my cabin. What can I tell her? She wouldn't understand that some people just don't want to get better. They rot slowly, infecting everyone around them by their sheer presence.

I think of a time long ago, when I had clung to my mother's dress and asked her, 'Mamma, is Daddy sick?'

'A little, yes.'

'Then let's take Daddy to a doctor.'

'Daddy will get okay,' she had said in a resigned voice.

I had persisted with the bursting exuberance of an eight-year-old. 'He's always falling and hurting himself. We have to go to the doctor!'

'We can't go to the doctor, Johnny!' she had cried with real anguish in her voice. 'Then everyone will think your daddy is a bad man!'

'Daddy is a bad man! He screams at me and shouts at you. I hate him!'

She couldn't explain to me that men from respected, well-to-do families did not become alcoholics. If they did, it was kept a closely guarded secret, spoken about in hushed tones. Else, the wife and the child became objects of their pity, while the husband was made out to be a monster. It never occurred to anyone that it was merely an addiction and needed to be treated like any other illness.

I cannot put into words my mother's desperate state of mind, to be neglected and abused by her husband, accused and held guilty by her in-laws and relatives for not doing enough to save her husband from a life of ruin. Most of all, to be forbidden from seeking outside help to cure her husband's deteriorating mind. She bottled it all up, shrinking into herself. It was the build-up of all that anguish that finally led to her death on the cold bathroom floor on a freezing winter night.

When Thy Will came to me after Father's death, I vowed to help people like my mother. For all the advancement in science, not much has changed; families are still ashamed to admit that they have an alcoholic or a drug addict in the family.

Thy Will is my answer to the poor-rich, the famous and the well respected who can't or won't walk into a general hospital and say that they have an addiction problem, or that their father, husband or son is an addict.

The task only becomes difficult with these new-age drugs competing with my old enemy, alcohol. It's an uphill battle, which I intend to win any way I can. If it means resorting to blackmail, so be it.

The phone rings. It's Mira.

'Johnny, where are you?'

'At work.'

'Why aren't you answering my calls? I left a dozen messages with that dumb-wit secretary.'

'Hey, Sera's sharp as a blade.'

'Screw her, Johnny.'

'I wish.'

'What's gotten into you?'

'Sorry, having a bad day at work.'

'Will you meet me for dinner tonight? I'll cook.'

'Sure, I'll be there by seven.'

'Johnny, I have something to tell you.'

'Confession time, huh?'

That is the wrong thing to say and she slams the receiver down. I wonder who sent her that note and the orchids, and why did she look like she was hiding something?

I hope to god she isn't cheating on me. Then I remember the message on Sera's tee this morning, 'LoVE KilLs'.

It is seven and a single lamp flickers to highlight the tastefully done living room. Money has not just been spent lavishly but wisely. Mira's flat on the second floor is visible even to an uninterested onlooker on the street below at night. I run up the stairs instead of taking the lift and feel the adrenalin rush as I press the buzzer and wait.

No answer. I press the buzzer a second, a third and a fourth time. I bang at the door hard; no sound.

I sit in my car, staring hard at the lamp flickering in her

living room. There is a puzzling stillness in the damp air. The heaviness grows, reminding me of the night Mom died. I was the first one to find her. She lay like a lifeless doll, clad in a pink wool nightgown, eyes and mouth agape, as if her screams had died in her throat. I remember shaking her really hard, crying, 'Mamma, wake up.' It was a Sunday morning, the only day she allowed me to watch cartoons on TV all day long. I remember thinking, why did Mamma have to die on a Sunday. I missed all the cartoons that day and the Sunday after that and every other Sunday till Papa died. He hated the sound of TV in the house. Mamma had taken all the fun with her.

I consider the possibility that our relationship is over and that, once again, I am alone.

I take out my sketchbook from the dashboard and draw Mira as I had first met her, dead to the world.

Diary of an Alcoholic

Johnny had a little rabbit,
Mira had a fucking habit,
Rabbit died, Mira lied, Johnny cried!

The rhyme echoed again and again till I could catch every single word that fell from that crooked mouth. In the pale yellow light, the predatory movement contrasted with the quarry's still, death-like form.

Though life pulsated in her, it was ebbing.

Her eyelids fluttered. The drug had already begun to weave its gentle magic. My drink remained untouched; my hands did not shake, neither did my body crave that one drink to pull myself together. Not tonight. The drama was unfolding right in front of my eyes and I did not want to miss a single thing.

A fly buzzed around excitedly; maybe the tiny creature could smell death. God only knows what these fucking animals and insects are capable of. The fly swatter came down with force and so did the butcher's knife from the kitchen.

As far as my eyes could see, like so many other things and people in her life, the knife too was just a fucking showpiece!

Johnnys of the World

What a waste. The young women had the most beautiful eyes I had ever seen in my fifteen years in the murder business.

Most murder victims looked frightful in death. Their eyes were filled with pain, fright or surprise, their bodies battered, mutilated, awkwardly sprawled in an unbecoming angle.

But this lady here was graceful in death, at ease. The dreamy look in her eyes was what made me suspect that she had overdosed on some deadly drug.

She looked lovely in a white silk dress, a dash of red on her lips from the wine she had been sipping. There was only one glass, which meant she had been drinking alone, but not necessarily. Killers are known to rinse their glass quite thoroughly before letting themselves out.

The case was simple, the open-and-shut kind, but daughters of wealthy and powerful people don't just drop dead. They die dramatic, headline-grabbing deaths because their families just won't drop the case.

So, here I am in a tastefully done apartment, checking for fingerprints, going through personal effects, trying to catch a killer who may just be a figment of the mourning father's imagination.

Kaizad Kermani is a man known for making generous political donations. His daughter is lying cold on the settee. 'Wrap it up ASAP, Ray!' – that was the police commissioner's briefing when I had left Ooty for the rich man's paradise, Monele.

The press was already calling it 'The Kermani Killing'; speculation was rife. How could a beautiful and successful business woman be on drugs and hide it from her family and associates? She was, after all, closing million-dollar deals on a daily basis. Her father believed that the apple of his eye was not a druggie. I was sure that the autopsy report would prove him wrong, but I did not have the heart to say that to the man.

I have seen some brilliant scamsters, artists, movie stars and executives leading ordinary lives, doing extraordinary work, sniffing white powder, rolling a rizla or simply swigging the expensive malt. My previous posting in the heartland of Chennai's political families and Tamil film industry had taught me much.

I smoked a cigarette, impatiently waiting for my men to photograph the body and bundle it to be taken to the city morgue for an autopsy. Suddenly, the fat constable on duty brought my attention to a sketch lying in a corner under the settee. The sketch was perfect in every way, every tiny detail of the murder scene was on paper: the wilted orchids placed across her midriff, the knife balanced precariously on the low table and her dreamy eyes.

Surely, the dead girl couldn't have drawn herself and then quietly gone and overdosed. I decided to look more closely this time and attacked her phone book with renewed zeal.

One name leapt out from the pages, doing its ugly dance.

I dialled the number and it rang seven times before a groggy voice answered. 'Hello.'

'Is that Johnny Will?'

'Hmm . . .'

'How do you know Mira?'

'She's my fiancée.' The voice was suddenly very awake. 'Who's this again?'

'Are you aware that she was found dead this morning in her apartment?'

'Asshole, I don't scare that easily, I saw her last night.'

With that the phone was disconnected. Withholding my name is hardly police etiquette but I wanted to catch him off guard, gauge his reaction and at the back of my mind there was this fear that he might recognize my name as I had recognized his. I was excited at the prospect of meeting him, the boy who had challenged me to find him guilty of his father's death. I couldn't.

There was no evidence, at least nothing that was admissible in court. My superior refused to base the case on flimsy evidence such as the sketch of a man burnt to death. I guess old habits are hard to kick, though looking at Johnny's present sketch, I'd say his art has greatly improved from when he was a fat fifteen-year-old.

Our coffee is getting cold and there's a fly licking the rim of my bone-china cup, but I dare not put it to my lips with the grieving father struggling to keep his emotions under check. Sitting in Kermani's mansion overlooking the mountains, I can think of no good reason why a wealthy heiress like Mira Kermani would want to marry scum like Johnny fat boy.

'We found her blood stream full of morphine.'

'But morphine is a pain reliever. Why would my daughter take morphine?'

'Morphine is an analgesic, yes, but it's also known to cause dependence when taken frequently. Your daughter died of an overdose of morphine, which caused respiratory depression. She injected herself to death.'

'My daughter wasn't a junkie! She couldn't stand syringes. She was scared of them.'

I noted that down, it was important. If Mira was scared of syringes, why would she choose morphine which had to be injected intramuscularly? Also, there were no needle marks on her body to show frequent use or dependence on morphine. On the other hand, her doctor-fiancé had easy access to this particular drug. That brought me to the next important question.

'Since when has your daughter been engaged to Dr Johnny Will?'

'That's nonsense! My daughter was never engaged to anybody, Officer Ray.'

'According to my information, they have been in a steady relationship for three years.'

'My daughter did some tax work for Johnny's facility and may have had a relationship, but it wasn't serious.'

'What makes you say that, Mr Kermani?'

'We Kermanis marry our own and Mira knew it better than anyone else.' His voice was steel.

I could believe that.

'What do you think of Johnny Will?'

'Is Johnny involved in my daughter's death, Officer?'

'At this point I am exploring all possibilities.'

'He's a smart enough boy doing some good work. Mira certainly thought the world of him.'

'What did you think, Mr Kermani?'

'I don't think he killed my daughter. He's too smart for that.'

It was not what I wanted to hear, but Kermani was not a fool. A shrewd businessman, he certainly had the ability to size up a man his daughter was seeing.

'Can you think of anyone who might want to harm her, any romantic liaison?'

'No, she was highly ambitious. She hung out with a lot of people, but wasn't really into anybody.'

The daughter who was not really into anybody was two months' pregnant when she died. A twenty-first-century woman didn't get pregnant if she didn't want to. There was a story there. But first, I had to tell Kermani that his daughter had committed the original sin.

'It can't be! She would have told me. We were very close,' he said with the crumbling confidence of a man who had reared a child with love and affection only to lose her to an unforeseen enemy, adulthood. Tears streamed down his face. He didn't bother to wipe them or turn his face away; the proud man was past caring.

Lines from 'A Lesser-known Poet' came to mind as I saw him sobbing quietly.

The heart that sobs a thousand deaths,
And curses God for not taking him first,
Can only belong to a bereaved father.

The Vulture's Feast

The traditional white muslin dress fluttered around her ankles, her body scrubbed clean. She lay on a marble slab surrounded by the elements: earth, water, fire, ether, air and fresh flowers.

The Parsi high priests performed her last rites in the Tower of Silence before her body was placed in an open iron casket. A road snaked uphill and stopped abruptly at the entrance to a lush green forest; neither priests nor relatives followed beyond this point.

The casket, carried on the shoulders of the corpse bearers, was placed in the Dakhma, a raised circular structure where her body was stripped of every bit of the white muslin and offered to the vultures. The last act of charity by a mortal – to feed hungry birds who would gorge on the flesh.

The vulture's feast was yesterday, and no, I wasn't there to say goodbye to Mira. No outsider was allowed at the funeral; the Parsis had their own set customs.

I mourned for Mira as I watched her body being wheeled out of her house. A reporter narrated the juicier details in a baritone, telecasting the event live, even as police officials zoomed in and out of the frame.

My mind did not want to think of the why and how; it just kept going back to the past.

Most men don't care what the woman sleeping next to them looks like in the morning. But I had studied her face from every angle, the slack mouth, the serene features, the flutter of an eyelash, all so beautiful in the morning light. Not a trace of the night's wild frenzy or the insatiable thirst.

She duped me with her vile ways, now I knew what she meant when she said, 'Johnny, I need to feel alive, I need to be loved but you can't always give me both.'

The mist was beginning to clear.

Somehow I had to find the resources to go on. There was work to be done, patients to be seen and questions to be answered.

I did not know then that my life would become a series of jumbled Q&A sessions run by a man I had insulted long ago.

'I don't see any need for formalities, Johnny. I am an old acquaintance, am I not?' Officer Ray had barged into my office earlier, and now reclined in the chair as if it were his own.

It took me a while to place him. He looked quite distinguished now. The thick-lens, rimless glasses added to his stature, almost announced a brain at work.

'You seem to have lost all that baby fat. Nice. Can't say the same about your face, though. Positively hideous.'

'How can I help, Officer Ray?'

'Why doesn't Kermani know about your engagement to Mira?'

'We were waiting for the right time to tell him. She thought he'd go ballistic. You see, Officer, Parsis only marry among themselves.'

'I have heard that before. Where were you the night . . .'

'She invited me for dinner but wasn't home when I knocked around seven, so I decided to wait for her in my car.'

'A neighbour heard you bang her door quite loudly. Were you angry with her about something?'

'Even if I were angry, I wouldn't make a public display of it at her doorstep and then go kill her, would I?'

'That's exactly what someone as smart as you would do; the very neighbours who saw you would then become your alibi. And on the phone you did admit that you saw her.'

The odd phone call now made sense.

'I lied.'

'Now, why would you lie about something like that, Johnny?'

'I thought it was a disgruntled patient trying to get a rise out of me.'

He was quiet for a moment and then asked very politely if he could have some coffee. I inferred two things from his tone: one, he had a few incriminating aces up his sleeves, and two, he was going to be here for a while.

'How did you meet Mira?'

'She looked after the financial side of my business venture.'

'What about her drug problem?'

'She didn't have any, an occasional thing, but that was over long back.'

'But we found traces of morphine in her body. How come you didn't detect signs of drug abuse, considering you do this for a living?'

'There weren't any signs, Officer.'

To some, drugs open the gates to a gravity-free world that is a kaleidoscope of bright colours, bizarre visions and muted echoes. To others they bring an awakening, a craving for flesh and all the forbidden pleasures the world has to offer. To Mira, it was both. I was ashamed to admit it, so I didn't.

'How long did you wait in the car?'

'Why, Officer, you must already know that, nosey neighbours are such a delight.'

'You left at nine, two hours later.'

'Right.'

'According to the autopsy report, 200 mg of morphine was given to her around eight and she died an hour later. The same time you conveniently claim to have left for home without seeing her. She was at home, dying in her living room. Any ideas why she didn't open the door for you?'

When I didn't reply, he presented me with a page out of my sketchbook.

'Where did you find this?'

'Under Mira's settee and that's exactly how we found her.' He pointed at the sketch.

I looked closely at it. I had indeed drawn it.

'I don't know how it got under her settee.'

'Surely the sketch didn't just walk up to her apartment.'

He decided to change his line of questioning. 'Tell me, were you the father of the child she was carrying?'

It was said very casually.

'She was pregnant?' I choked on the question.

'Two months. I am surprised you didn't know about it.'

I waited for the blood to clear my head before I replied. 'I think she wanted to tell me . . .'

'What do you think, Johnny? What happened to her? Did she kill herself and her baby or did she have some help?'

'I can't think!' I turned away from him to stare at the white wall.

'I am really sorry about the child.'

He stood up and left the room.

I flung the brass paperweight, suddenly aware of my loneliness and of what I had lost – faith. If I had told him the child wasn't mine, Officer Ray would have had an easy case against me: 'Doctor kills fiancée in a fit of jealous rage.'

I was jealous of the man who had lured Mira away from me and enraged because he had taken her forever. My memories would forever be tainted, her betrayal an ugly scar on my soul.

SERA

Lovelorn

Reforming addicts is not always rewarding; there are those who disgust you to the core. Like this swarthy guy with a lisp. I dread his appointments; they drain me of all that is good and positive in me. He leers at me like a rich man driving through a red-light district.

It's all very subtle, nothing I can complain to Johnny about. So, I suffer through these bi-monthly sessions, hoping he'll get better and leave. But he never does. He promptly comes in for his psychotherapy session and enjoys every minute of it, making me uncomfortable.

'Could Johnny fit me in today, Sera?'

'I am afraid not, Mr Sarkar. He's occupied.'

'I wanted to discuss my medication; this one's not helping much.'

'Just give it some time.'

'I wanted to pay my condolences too. I saw the news. They are making a big thing of his girlfriend's murder. It must have come as a terrible shock.'

Noticing the stiffening of my shoulders, the bastard leant forward and brought his face close to mine.

'Someone's loss is someone's gain, what say, doll?'

I ignored the remark and with great composure said, 'We'll see you next Saturday, Mr Sarkar.'

He smiled, blew me an air kiss and went out, whistling.

The jerk was a famous theatre actor. Between snorting coke and running a gay casting couch, he had won a couple of international awards. And he had a sharp nose for when a woman had the hots for a man.

I adore Johnny. I had, since the first day I started working here. Sometimes I get mixed signals from him, but I was kidding myself. To make it easier on myself, I think my failed first marriage is what bothered him.

It's difficult to sit in the recliner opposite him every morning and discuss patients and treatments when all I want is to kiss those lips. He has a surgeon's fingers, lean and sensitive and I have a thousand fantasies surrounding them. All of this is in my mind and that's where it is going to stay.

I would never have thought Johnny would be capable of deceiving his patients. If Zac is to be believed, Johnny's childhood has a lot to do with the decisions he makes in the present.

Restless, I decided to take a walk in the rose garden that I had revived last winter. Johnny agreed readily as the garden in full bloom reminded him of happier days when his mother was alive. So often, after he returns from a good game of golf, he joins me in the garden and helps me water the plants. He's a strange man, indifferent to people and their feelings in so many ways, yet there runs a thread of vulnerability under that veneer of nonchalance – and that is what tugs at my heart.

Even though I knew he was spoken for, Johnny is my

fantasy lover. With Mira dead, the probability of that becoming a reality had suddenly doubled.

It is callous of me to think like that when Johnny was grieving for his mate like a dangerously wounded animal. But Mira always treated me as a lowly employee not worth her attention or acknowledgement. Her abrupt conversations in person had not endeared her much to me. 'Is Johnny in?' she'd demand. Then, without waiting for a reply, she would barge in while he was in a session with a patient. Johnny never let his annoyance show; in fact he always treated her with the smile specially reserved for her. Was I jealous!

I didn't wish her dead . . . just gone from Johnny's life. Now she was, and I didn't know how to comfort him. He'd retreated into a shell. I wished he would speak to someone, Zac or me.

The moment this thought crossed my mind, Zac's Omni turned into the driveway. He wasn't alone. Adele Will, Johnny's aunt, had come along to offer her condolences. Dressed in her customary black, an A-line, round-collared cotton dress, with white lace trimmings around the cuffs, she appeared daintier than ever. The silver belt around her tiny waist and black pumps made her look like a college girl. There was a hint of summer pink on her lips, dark mascara and kohl turning upward at the corners. She didn't look made-up; she looked lovely, still stuck in the seventies.

'Good evening, Sera. How's our boy holding up?'

'Not too good, Ms Will.'

'We'll see.'

We stood there in an uncomfortable silence. Zac asked if Johnny would see them, to which Adele Will replied in her no-nonsense tone, 'Of course, he will. What a silly thing to say? We are the only family he has left.'

I was not sure Johnny would be happy to see them, though. He had not shown much inclination to see his aunt in the past. I left them in the garden and went in search of Johnny to the new building where the patients were housed.

It was time for the evening rounds, and Johnny never missed it come rain or storm.

There he was, speaking to a patient in a soothing tone, telling him to relax. Not many people knew this, but Johnny was a dab hand at hypnosis. I was most certain that the tapes were merely the tip of the iceberg. Whatever information Johnny needed, he got it merely by flexing his fingers. Those beautiful fingers!

In the nineties, hypnosis was still new in India. In fact, until a few years ago, the medical fraternity considered it a dubious practice. Now there were those who swore by it. Johnny used it often to dwell deep into the patient's mind, often achieving a breakthrough when traditional therapy and medicine failed.

The patient crawled into bed, pulled his sheet up and promptly fell asleep. Lately, I had been having strange dreams of Johnny playing god and his rapid downfall from the seat of heaven. And now, there was a strange smile on his face, a godlike smile just like the one in my dreams. I stood there, indecisively. Would Johnny's puppets be his downfall? There were already rumours of his involvement in Mira's death.

I must have been staring unseeingly for a while, because the next thing I knew, Johnny was shaking me by the hands.

'What's wrong, Sera?'

'Nothing, I just came to tell you that Zac and Ms Will are waiting to see you . . . I could ask them to go.'

'Ask Aunt Adele to go?'

He let out a strange laugh and started walking towards the rose garden. In my hurry to keep up, I missed a step and lost my balance.

I had imagined it a thousand times: Johnny would catch me in his arms in the nick of time. No such luck, I fell hard on the floor and found myself flat on the ground.

Another fantasy down the drain. He really didn't like me as much as I sometimes thought he did. He never made any attempt to touch me, which was a sign enough that he wasn't interested. But my body is on fire every time he comes near.

Halfway to the garden, Johnny insisted that I go to the kitchen and request Marie to fix us tea and some snacks.

The kitchen smelled of chicken broth and caramel custard. Slowly the trays started to pile up. It was time to feed the rich, the famous and the oh-so-neurotic! An orderly carried the trays to the patient's wing.

'Marie, can you please prepare tea and something to munch? Johnny has guests.'

'Who would that be?'

Marie had been the cook at the Will household for forty-seven years and knew all the dead Wills, their secrets and the skeletons in their closets.

The only problem was that she wasn't much of a talker. Every time I tried to chat her up about Johnny's childhood, she clamped up like a self-sacrificing patriot. Such was her loyalty to the master of the house.

Fifteen minutes later, I walked back to the garden with another silver tray bearing four cups of tea, coconut cookies and butter biscuits.

All eyes were on me as I walked up to them. There was no

conversation, only the faint sound of the evening breeze and a patient moaning in pain far away. I realized that despite Adele Will's tall claims of being Johnny's family, Johnny had none.

Watching him in that moment, I fell head over heels for that man, as he stared at the lonely swell of the mountains, reflecting the last light of the evening sun. My face must have mirrored my feelings for I felt Adele's gaze on me. Her eyes alight with the cunning she tried so hard to hide.

'Come, my dear, we have all been waiting for Marie's delightful cookies and butter biscuits.'

I was surprised she knew exactly what was on the tray, but then I remembered that this was Adele's home too, long ago, until she was disinherited and then later tossed out by Johnny. I didn't know why, and even Zac refused to answer that question. In fact, he became rather jittery when asked about his mother and his cousin.

We sipped our tea in silence. Then Adele said, 'You should get married now, Johnny. You turn – what – thirty-four come January. It's time Thy Will is filled with the noise of little ones. Don't you agree, Sera?'

She looked at me pointedly. I blushed under her direct gaze.

Johnny's jaw clenched, but he continued staring at the impassive hills.

Without giving it much thought, I said, 'I agree, Ms Will. Both the house and the master need a mistress's touch.'

If I was angling for a reaction, I certainly got one as Johnny fixed his brown eyes on my face and said, 'Would you be up to the challenge, Sera?'

I was stumped and mumbled a faint, 'I uh . . . just meant,' letting out a hollow laugh.

Johnny got up and said a curt, 'Good night then' to no one in particular and walked back to the house. We stared at his retreating back, straight and proud, as he disappeared from our sight.

Yes, I longed to be the mistress of this formidable house and its lonely master. If Mira's measured affection could turn Johnny's head, my selfless love could surely capture his bleeding heart.

But is selfless love what Johnny wanted?

For five long years, I had stayed with an ageing, boring husband because I did not have it in me to face the world alone. I was afraid of being alone, of being poor and most importantly of not having someone to look after me. I gave what a man needs, a warm body in his bed and food on the table, and in return got the security of his name and a luxurious home. I am not Mira – an independent, self-possessed woman. I am the exact opposite.

The truth is I have never known what it is like to have a man love me; I have always been the slave in a relationship. I want what Mira had with Johnny, only better, and her death might just do that for me.

Mistress of the House

A visit from Adele always sets me brooding; it triggers memories of a time that is best forgotten. A hot water shower later, I am still pacing my room.

There was a time the whole family used to have tea in the garden.

Grandpa Will liked to sip his tea from a saucer, blowing at it to cool it. Adele would be bent over her canvas, Mother absorbed in her cross-stitch, while Father stared far away at the hills as if burdened by them. The great burden of guilt.

One evening, Father gathered the courage to confess to Mother that he had been sleeping with another woman; he called her 'a lady' whom he had fallen in love with. The initial attraction had given way to love. But the love that had come easily had gone as easily, like an irritation in the nose that turns into a sneeze. He now wanted to come back to Mother and make things work. Mother became hysterical, and started banging her head against the wall till it bled.

Marie had tried to console her, but in vain, her pain was acute, her faith in tatters and the will to live left her.

She even attempted a lame suicide with a few sleeping

pills that proved to be ineffective; father's tear glands went into overdrive.

Accusations and promises flowed back and forth. She wanted to castrate him.

She asked, what was the need to confess, to crawl back to her now?

The answer was simple – guilt. But the self-sacrificing bastard didn't have it in him to confess to the whole truth. He could only tell her that he was sorry for breaking his vows and that his conscience was eating away at him. He wanted to do the right thing. He wanted their marriage to work. He loved her, he said, over and over until they both believed it to be true.

Of course, he never did tell her that he could never be with her the way he was with 'the lady', that his own wife could never evoke such emotions in him, never would.

Yet, he chose peace of mind over a piece of ass and crawled back to Mother. It was a patchwork job to assuage his guilt, and it worked, at least for a while.

Mother had no choice but to believe him. He wailed like a child, grovelled to be forgiven. She gave in, clung on to him. What else was there to cling on to? They had been married only a year. Men strayed, but had he not come back to her? That meant his feelings for her were stronger than his lust for that woman. He didn't love that woman. The love he fleetingly felt for the other woman was just his excuse for screwing her. She couldn't take that excuse away from him.

My foolish mother just wanted him back, so she never questioned why he fell in love with another woman in the first place and why he fell out of it so quickly?

No one wanted to know the whys, least of all the husband

and wife clinging to each other in the face of this emotional avalanche. By the time the answers came, four or five years had passed.

So, two lonely people came together again, and I was born a year later. An aftermath of two adults wanting to make a go at their marriage; like all things, even the euphoria of having a baby didn't last long. Mother realized the futility of it all, how could she pluck the fragile flower called 'love' when it didn't grow in her yard in the first place.

He drifted away, despite all her efforts.

Marie had told me once, 'Your father tried, Johnny. He tried till it broke him, but what could the poor man do? His heart was not in it.'

A year after I was born. Adele gave birth to Zac, the bastard son.

Adele took it all with her head held high and chin up, and even when Grandpa Will disinherited her and the newborn, she did not disclose the name of the father. The sham that was my parent's marriage continued, till I saw Adele and my father together when I was five. The pale, unhealthy flesh of his buttocks glistened with sweat in the dim light of the bulb. They lay in the dusty basement doing their dark deed, while the sun shone bright outside. The coarse hair on his body rubbed against her taut torso.

From where I stood, I could see her pointed nipple grazing his ear. She looked like a dainty flower pressed under him, or a fruit, perhaps, as he sucked at her mouth as if it were a juicy mango. To a five-year-old, the sight of two naked adults – his father and his aunt – feasting on each other was a sickening one. The image of their coupling remains etched on my mind to this day.

The identity of the woman father had been screwing, came as a shock to Mother, but what hurt her even more was that he had been doing it under the same roof. Zac was four years old by then.

Their loveless marriage and constant bickering drove Father to the bottle. Mother, in her bitterness and zeal to punish, refused to release him from his vows. Months turned into slow, meaningless years, till Father found her dead in the bathroom. A few more years crawled; the worst years of my life, and then the bastard burnt to death. I sincerely believe that, at the time of his death, he loved nobody; he was incapable of it.

Adele remains more dead than alive, she has been used all her life. As the other woman, her role had been to fill his bed, father his child and bear the disgrace of being a loose woman. Adele was the filth in everyone's eyes and my father was never man enough to set it right.

Today, for the first time I thought of Aunt Adele's life. I wondered how things would have been if instead of doing the right thing, Father would have chosen wrong, chosen Adele. I hated her most days, but lying on the bed, brooding over life and its twisted jokes, I saw a lonely, badly scarred woman.

This one time, when I was thirteen, Father was drunk and in a mood to fight. I hurled abuses at him, thinking he wouldn't be able to run after me in his drunken state.

'You drunkard! Living in my mother's house, on my mother's money!'

Father took me by surprise and chased me to the large hall with a golf club in his hand. He would have smashed my head had Adele not intervened in time. She pushed him away and took the club out of his hand. She slapped him and called him a 'wimp'. Shamed, he crawled back into his study to drink some more.

She knelt beside me on the floor and said not too unkindly, 'Whatever his weaknesses may be, Johnny, he's your father. Don't be so hard on him.' She patted my head and left.

I hadn't seen that Adele again. Time had only made her more and more bitter towards me.

Adele, Robin, Daisy. The love triangle never did end right for anyone, because no one found it in their heart to step up or give way to love. As a child, I never could understand their need to carry on with the façade of being a family.

But that is how the world lives, in charades of loving families, no one acknowledging that all is not well and never will be. A beautiful patchwork of lies is what we create to fit in.

The Players

A knock on the heavily carved door and an impatient young woman appeared, ready to leave for work. I had no choice but to detain her by flashing my badge and explaining my reason for being there.

'Anna, or should I call you Ananya, Mr Kermani tells me you were good friends with Mira since your school days at Lovedale.'

'Anna. We were thick.'

'Thick enough to do recreational drugs together?'

'Absolutely not, Officer!'

'Tell me about her pregnancy.'

'She was pregnant? Oh my god!'

'I thought you said you were best friends.'

'We were not that kind of friends. She didn't confide in me.'

'My vocabulary fails me, tell me what kind of friends were you then?'

'Officer, after college, money was tight and Mira got me a job at her father's resort. She never let me forget that I was on her father's payroll. So, pardon me, if this doesn't fit into your definition of friendship.'

'How would you describe her?'

'Rich, spoilt, brilliant.'

'What about her feelings for Johnny?'

'Feelings? Um, she thought he was quite the stud in bed. She liked him, I guess, there was nothing more to it.'

Later that day, I could only think about what the world had come to. What had happened to good old friendships, the kind where friends knew each other's joys and sorrows? I have a fifteen-year-old daughter and I shudder at the thought of her becoming this 'Anna' person, talking casually about sleeping with men.

I decided the sex talk I meant to have with my daughter when she turned seventeen might have to come sooner. Sitting in my veranda sipping tea, I looked at the Kermani case from a fresh angle.

Why was there no one to support Johnny's claim that he and Mira were engaged? Forget the engagement, no one even remotely believed that they had something of a serious relationship.

Her father didn't think so and her best friend had ripped apart Johnny's touching claims of love. Only Johnny believed that Mira was in love with him.

Could it be that Mira had accidentally got pregnant and had wanted to get rid of the lovechild, while Johnny opposed her decision and badgered her to marry him? Maybe Mira was adamant on an abortion while Johnny wanted a family? That would be a good enough motive for Johnny to kill Mira, hadn't Johnny killed his father for much less?

A fresh start demanded fresh legwork in the fox's lair. I checked my list; it was time to interview the embittered aunt, the underdog cousin and the young assistant.

I am one of the best investigating officers on the force. I have a couple of commendations under my belt and I didn't get them by the usual means, kissing ass.

I worked hard, solved every case that came my way and didn't stop to make friends on my way up, so I really didn't have too many people poking their nose in my business. The early-morning drive to Monele lasted fifty minutes, and the beauty of the clouded mist kissing the narrow roads turned out to be a great distraction for my over-burdened mind.

The luxury villas on the outskirts are breathtaking, but the real attraction is the town centre, which has retained its old-world charm, with makeshift cobblestone streets, small cafés and patisseries run by locals – nothing fancy, just wooden tables and benches. I parked my Jeep and walked over to Café Aspen.

It seemed busy and well maintained. I noticed the self-service sign, and went to give my order for coffee and a cheese sandwich to a lady preoccupied with her morning accounts.

Without even looking up, she asked me to go to some other café. A customer so early in the morning clearly was not welcome here. I studied her closely. She must have been a striking beauty in her day, still looked quite young, in fact. It was evident in the tilt of her chin and those slanted eyes – this was a timeless face. My research had not prepared me for this. The old hag had turned out to be a beauty, and in my books, beauty beckoned trouble.

I walked back to the Jeep and searched for old family pictures in the file of Robin Muthanna, my first case. There they were, all the Wills in happier times, the year 1977.

The black-and-white picture only enhanced the beauty

of Adele Will. But what caught my attention was the slight figure of Daisy Will, Johnny's mother and Adele's elder sister. A woman with a pained face, she seemed to merge into the background, seeming dull in the presence of her beautiful younger sister. I jotted down the question uppermost in my mind: why had a beautiful woman like Adele remained unmarried? Definitely not for the dearth of suitors. And who had fathered the bastard she had refused to put up for adoption?

Lines from 'A Lesser-known Poet' came to mind:

If Love could be bought,
The queue would be long.

These questions didn't seem to have anything to do with Mira Kermani's death, but to me they were an important piece of a jigsaw. Without delay, I flashed my badge to intimidate the woman behind the counter.

'Adele Will, I am Officer Ray, here to question you about the death of Mira Kermani and Robin Muthanna.'

Her startled glance at the mention of Robin's name convinced me that it had been a mistake not to question her all those years ago. But a rookie officer didn't have much say in those days, especially when it seemed like an open-and-shut case to the superior officer.

'I don't understand . . . what does Johnny's father have to do with Mira's death?'

'I am just trying to get a handle on Johnny Will, his childhood, his father's death and everything in between.'

She seemed to relax visibly, and rose from behind the counter to place a sandwich and a cup of coffee in front of me. I was impatient to start the questioning, so I ate the sandwich in two bites and quaffed the scalding coffee.

'Why didn't you ever get married?'

'Thirty years ago, men didn't want a woman who had living proof that she had slept with another man.'

'Who was this man?'

'No one worth remembering, Officer.' It was said very calmly, but I didn't believe her.

'A woman doesn't forget the father of a child, Ms Will.'

'No, she doesn't, but it does get a little confusing if you have slept with too many.'

Her reply had me tongue-tied, I had not expected her to be so flippant.

'Your sister let you stay at Thy Will after your father expired and the house passed on to her. How did you feel about that?'

'Grateful. Wouldn't you, if you had no money, no roof over your head and an illegitimate child to feed?'

'Tell me what Robin and Daisy's marriage was like?

'Boring, like all marriages.'

'Why did a promising cartoonist like Robin become an alcoholic?'

'I wouldn't know.'

'You lived in the same house; you must have noticed when a sober, intelligent man began to drink?'

'Maybe his wife drove him to it!'

Her laughter bellowed all the way outside; curious locals peeped in. Had she envied her plain sister, with the beautiful house and the famous husband? And most of all, did she resent the charity meted out to her in the house that was her birthright as well?

'Why did Johnny throw you and Zac out after Robin's death?'

'Why he threw us out is something you have to ask Johnny. Want my opinion? He's just a greedy boy, always has been!'

'In what way?'

'Greedy for control, Johnny likes to control situations, people and even their emotions. It doesn't work that way.' When I didn't say anything, she added, 'You can't make people love you.'

'Were Mira and Johnny serious about marriage?'

'Johnny, maybe, Mira couldn't care less.'

'Why?'

'No, woman wants half a man in her life . . . her bed, not for long.'

The tape recorder in my pocket was recording every word, I decided to mull over this remark later.

'Is Johnny the possessive type?'

'Oh, yes, the possessive–aggressive type, if you want my opinion.'

'You think he could have killed Mira in cold blood?'

'Who knows what lengths a man will go to, to keep the woman he loves by his side?'

The smile that spread on her face was similar to the one when she talked about her sister, the hatred for mother and son quite evident. Saying nothing and implying everything.

Zac

Crime in Knickers

I spanked Anna hard as I took her from behind. She normally enjoyed these sessions, but her heart was not in it today, nor was mine. I continued spanking anyway. Mother had done a thorough job of ruining my evening and I needed to get it out of my system. Some police officer had scared Mother witless by asking all the wrong questions, and she had been harping about it all day.

'Don't you blab anything to that officer that may land us in trouble.'

'Like what, Mother?' I had asked, just to see her squirm.

'Like why Johnny threw us out. Attempt to murder could get you a life sentence, even if the crime was committed in knickers.'

'Too bad they don't have any tough sentences for adultery, Mother.'

Her palm hit my face with the speed of lightning. 'I should have left you in the gutter like everyone expected me to. It's never too late, remember that, Zac.'

Her warning jangled in my ears and I spanked harder with each thrust. Anna rolled out from under me, tears swimming in her eyes. I tried to kiss her by way of an apology; she spat the word 'swine' at me and rushed to the bathroom.

Anna and I saw each other every now and then. Mira had introduced me to her at the Seven Seas where she worked as a PRO. I had bragged to her about Mother's little café, least expecting her to turn up.

To my horror, she did turn up and I had to introduce Mother to her. No prizes for surmising that they both took an instant dislike to each other. Good for me; that ruled out family dinners.

I like Anna. She's brazen in a very urbane kind of way. I put my arms around her waist as she emerged from the bathroom and pulled her to me. Her skin was cool from the water she had splashed on herself and it felt good to rest my clammy body against hers. She was angry, but she didn't push me away. I nibbled at her ear and gently stroked the inside of her thigh. She moaned and I felt myself growing hard again. This time she pushed me away and threw my boxers at me.

'Pack it up, Zac, you did enough damage for today.'

I tried explaining to her how Mother was throwing a fit about the routine questioning in Mira's death.

'Officer Ray. That's the guy who came to question me. Why would he question your mother? She rarely ever saw Mira,' Anna said, tying her hair.

I was a bit distracted as she was still moving about naked. She had a wide rear, firm and round, one that would put any south Indian starlet to shame. She gave me that look and I searched my brain for an answer.

'No, not Mira, he wanted to know about Johnny. It seems my brother is their number one suspect at the moment.'

'I am not surprised. He was asking about Johnny and Mira's relationship. I told him there wasn't one; it was more like a sleeping arrangement.'

'Why the hell would you say something like that, Anna?

'Grow up, Zac, that's exactly how it was and you know it.'

'All I know is that Johnny loved Mira and she happily wore his ring on her ring finger,' I said.

'Well, women are known to do crazy things with a child in their belly.'

The floor below my feet seemed to move. I pulled back from her. 'Mira was pregnant? Who told you that?'

'Officer Ray.'

'Fish!'

This was frigging complicated. I needed fresh air and my own depressing company. I left, promising to call her the next day.

I walked to the ruins of Adam's Edge, the valley that lay behind Thy Will balanced precariously close to a cliff made famous by a few jilted lovers throwing themselves off the steep valley. I sat on my favourite bench, thinking of the time when I had tried to kill Johnny and almost succeeded. At sixteen, I was big for my age, my mind a swirling pool of hatred brought to boil by my mother's scheming, nagging ways.

Uncle Robin's death marked the end of an allowance to Mother and she had to beg Johnny's lawyers for every penny. In those days, I was not just scared of her, I loved her as well.

She had, after all, stood by me, borne the insults, the taunts, the shame but had not given up on her bastard child. My eyes saw a proud woman reduced to desperation and poverty. One evening, fooled by her agony and pain, a crowbar in hand, masking my face with a gunny bag, I waited for Johnny to return home from playing; this was the shortcut we used to reach home from the football ground that was in the middle of the town.

I hit him with the crowbar as he neared and kept hitting his stomach, legs and groin. Johnny was a fat little boy and no match for my fury.

I had smashed the crowbar in his face, twisted it like a knife, taking out a chunk of flesh from under his jaw, missing the jugular by inches. Blood had spurted out with great force and my bravado gave way. I ran to the same place where I am sitting now, leaving Johnny to bleed to death. He didn't.

In their hurry to save Johnny, the doctors stitched the left side of his face rather crudely, leaving an ugly scar.

The plan to make Mother the heir to the Will fortune failed, but fate has its quirks. There would be no other heir either. The scar would heal in time and so would the other injuries, but unfortunately his left testis was damaged.

The major long-term side-effect of 'blunt testicular trauma' was infertility and it was irreversible.

Mother had broken the news with gaiety to Johnny. 'No more snakes are going to be swimming out of that pond.'

To a seventeen-year-old, the news that he can't have children is hardly heart-breaking and so, like everything else, he took it in his stride.

In those days I lived in constant fear of Johnny giving my name to the police. He did no such thing. He came out of the hospital two months later, a gaunt figure with a crude scar running along the jawline. Numerous operations had been unable to fix that. I stood at my window as he slowly wobbled into the house, supported by Marie.

'Why didn't you tell the police about me, Johnny?' I had asked him.

'I couldn't let my brother go to jail.'

I just looked at him dumbfounded. Had the same brother not beaten him to death?

'Zac, you want money, you can have it. It's half yours, anyway.'

Oh! Shame rose like nausea in my throat and I blurted out angrily, 'I don't want your charity, cousin!'

'We aren't cousins, Zac, we are half-brothers.'

'What does that mean?'

'We have the same father.'

Those words still echo in my sleep. I can never forget that forlorn look on Johnny's face. I slumped to the floor, in awe of my mother's lies and my father's treachery. It was there for all to see, the family scenes, the drinking.

Johnny and I had stared at each other for a long time. From that moment on, Johnny owned me.

He threw Mother out the next day. I was welcome to stay but I had already hung the albatross, my mother, around my neck by then.

'Zac Will?'

'Yes.'

'Officer Ray.'

I shook his outstretched hand warily. He ambushed me just as I was leaving Anna's flat after a heavy Sunday lunch and some wild, post-lunch coitus.

'Were they in love, Robin and Daisy Will?'

'Why are you so interested in my uncle and aunt?'

He thrust a black-and-white photograph in my hand. A family picture of when I was four. At first glance, we appeared to be a happy family; the only giveaway was Aunty Daisy's stooping shoulders and my father's heavy jowl and agitated eyes. I shrugged and gave it back to him. Mother, immaculate as ever, shone in the photograph, while Grandpa Will held Johnny, and I just sat on the floor unattended, uncared for.

'What do you want to know, Officer?'

'Why an intelligent, god-fearing Catholic hit the bottle and neglected his wife and child?'

'Can't help you there, Officer. I was only a child then, and not a very bright one, I'm afraid.'

His eyes challenged mine and I was the first to blink. I couldn't tell him that the pressure of having a wife and a mistress under the same roof could turn any man into an alcoholic.

'Johnny is a good artist, isn't he?'

He showed me a sketch of Mira dead on a settee.

'I am a good artist too,' I said.

'Are you saying you drew this sketch?'

'I am saying there are a lot of artists around, anyone could have drawn this.'

'So Johnny does have someone to stand up for him?'

'He can take care of himself, Officer.'

'I have a theory. Care to listen? I think Johnny killed Mira because she was too "free spirited" to marry him and have his child. By your own mother's admission, Johnny is a very "possessive–aggressive" male, and we all know how smart our man is.'

'Yes, but smart men don't murder their girlfriends to make them their wives.'

No reply was forthcoming and soon he left, handing over his business card. I tore the card in two and threw it away. I wouldn't need it, no matter how guilty Johnny appeared in the face of Officer Ray's bogus theory, bogus because that child wasn't Johnny's. Officer Ray only had to check Johnny's medical records to know.

But now the probability of Johnny killing Mira had doubled. An unfaithful woman could have tipped him over the edge, reminding him of his adulterous father.

Allergies

The table was decorated with apple strudel, chicken pies and freshly baked cilantro rolls from Sera's favourite baker. It was her idea to bring a little gaiety in the house by celebrating Marie's birthday. Marie had cut the carrot cake topped with whipped cream, chocolate flakes and tons of roasted nuts. It was the cake Mother would bake on my birthday every year. My mouth wouldn't stop watering at the sight of it.

'Cut the cake, Marie. I am salivating like Pavlov's dog!'

'Whose dog?'

Sera laughed; Zac and Marie obviously didn't get the joke.

'Never mind, just cut the cake.'

Zac began to sing the birthday song in his booming voice and we all joined in, when he suddenly stopped and asked her, 'Really, how old are you, Marie?'

Marie looked at him in mock horror and admonished, 'You never learnt any manners, Zac!'

At last, the cake was cut, hugs, kisses and presents went around. I had bought her another watch, Zac, a full makeover voucher from a plush salon, and Sera, a beautiful handmade shawl. Half an hour later, a tearful Marie cleared the table and thanked us all profusely.

'Did anyone hear that?' Sera stood up and urged us to listen. The emergency buzzer was ringing, growing stronger and clearer with each buzz. It had happened only once before and none of us wanted history to repeat itself.

We ran to the patients' ward and Zac asked Sunny, the head orderly, 'Who's dead?'

'No one, sir. A loose wire. The buzzer went off on its own.'

I felt dizzy with relief. The last time that buzzer had gone off, a patient had hung himself from the metal window by a rope fashioned out of bedsheets and pyjama bottoms; so severe was the pain of alcohol deprivation that he chose to end his life.

I walked to my cabin and shut the door, not wanting to be disturbed. My mind was full of ugly thoughts. Death seemed to be everywhere, amusing itself at my expense.

'Come in, Zac.' That forceful knock could only be Zac's.

'Are you alright, big brother?'

'I am fine.'

'It was a faulty connection, they are fixing it right away.'

Not in the mood to encourage conversation, I just mumbled a feeble, 'Super.'

Zac wasn't buying it. 'Johnny, you need to pull your act together. Some officer came around asking a lot of questions. He thinks the baby was yours, could it have been?'

'You should know better.'

'You wouldn't hurt her?'

'I wanted to hurt her very much, but the sad truth is she

was already dead by then. So I guess we'll never know if I would have acted on my impulse or not.'

Zac plugged his ears with his palms and said, 'Johnny, please, no more honest confessions.'

I couldn't help grinning at his concern for my well-being. After all, he would gain the most by my removal, Thy Will's assets would then belong to the illegitimate heir.

Grandpa Will was long dead, but he had made sure that no harm ever came to his precious house. In the event of my untimely demise or if I were to be a disgrace to the proud Will name, the house would go to my heir. Since I didn't have any, rather couldn't have any, Zac was next in line.

'Zac, relax! Don't worry about Ray, he's just an asshole who's got his own axe to grind.'

'Axe to grind?'

'He thinks I burnt our father to death. He was the officer-in-charge then.'

'Where did he get that ridiculous idea?'

'Umm, I think from the sketch you had drawn and dropped by Father's bedside.'

Zac leant against the wall for support. The memory of that dreadful night evoked strong emotions in both of us. We had never really spoken about it, about how we lifted our drunk father every other night from his own vomit or shit. Aunt Adele could hardly be called upon to clear the mess and Marie stayed a mile away from Father.

On a good day, we would find him naked and passed out in his bedroom. Needless to say, we never had any friends over, didn't want them to see Father doing the full monty.

Though Zac had not known the terrible secret of the sordid love triangle in those days, Robin had been the only father figure around. It was tougher on him, as Aunt Adele hardly ever found time to be a real mother.

In many ways, Zac was a very lonely boy. I felt bad for taunting him about the sketch. But like all lonely people, I have a funny way of expressing my feelings.

'Hey, Zac, I am sorry. The sketch means nothing.'

'No, it doesn't. I didn't hate him like you did.'

'That must be before you knew he had fathered you on the side.'

That remark made Zac really angry and his breathing became uneven. He grasped the sides of my swivel chair, forcing me to lean back and jammed his knee in my crotch.

'Next time you are planning to play your little mind games with me, Brother, remember that I know to hit where it hurts.'

That's how Sera found us.

'What's going on?'

'Oh, Zac's just been giving me a much-needed pep talk.'

Zac walked off in a huff, leaving a bewildered Sera staring in his direction.

'Were you and Zac fighting?'

'A brother-to-brother chat, that's all.'

'Could we have our weekly discussion now, Johnny?'

'Sure, I don't have anything scheduled for today.' Sera had the decency of not saying it out loud that there hadn't been any new appointments since the news of Mira's murder and my involvement had broken out.

We still had our inpatients and the old regulars, so there was no shortage of work.

'203 is responding to the treatment alright but his behaviour bothers me.'

'You are not supposed to be near 203. You know the rules.'

'I checked on him because you weren't around, and he was creating a ruckus to be let out in the yard. And he's pretty cute with that British accent.'

'Cute but deranged. Stay away from him.'

'He's been here before, hasn't he?'

'That's not your concern.' It came out too strongly and I rushed to make amends.

'Look, Sera, he almost got arrested in London for breaking glass on his girlfriend's face high on crystal meth. Keep that in mind the next time you are planning on playing Mary Poppins.'

'You know the police, Johnny, boyfriend's always prime suspect.'

'Point taken, Sera.'

I felt claustrophobic; it seemed like everyone was out to get me. I left her in my cabin – feeling guilty, I hope. She must have, for half an hour later, she came around to the study.

'Johnny, would you like to go out for dinner tomorrow night?'

'Super! Insulting people and then feeding them makes for an interesting apology.'

'Coming or not?'

'Sweetheart, just remind me tomorrow that we have a date.'

I wasn't likely to forget but it felt good to see Sera stalk out of the study all high and mighty.

After lunch, I opened the safe and took out the file of potentially the most dangerous patient at Thy Will.

Patient 203 was a heavy user of crystal meth, a drug

known to create an acute psychotic condition leading to extremely violent behaviour. Sera was right, this was his second visit, and this time he had outstayed his welcome and treatment.

He also suffered from a personality disorder called IED (intermittent explosive disorder), and needed psychiatric help apart from his drug problem. As a personal favour to his guardian, I couldn't or wouldn't discharge him. The British born and bred nephew of Kaizad Kermani had no plans of returning to London anytime soon.

His uncle doted on him like his own son and, with Mira dead, someone had to step up and take charge. Kermani believed that once the drugs were out of his system, he could introduce Azaan to the rest of the world as the scion of the Kermani clan.

He often said Azaan meant call to prayer and he was waiting for his prayers to be answered. In my personal and professional opinion, this man could only be a prayer in hell.

I am often wonderstruck at the ability of women to transform themselves into weapons of seduction. The revealing clothes, the painted lips, the intense perfume and that enticing look. Such were Sera's vibes that I hesitated to join her at the table she had booked at the 'Greasy Grill'. They made my favourite greasy steak. The ambience replicated an American diner in the middle of nowhere.

I went in and came out wondering what I was getting myself into. She probably imagined herself in love and was out to give all she had. I would be a fool to miss what was on offer. That was my smart self. My dumb self contradicted me, 'You pluck a bud and there will be consequences.'

As always, I ignored the dumb voice in my head and went in to taste the delights the evening had to offer.

'Sera, you look lovely in green.'

'Thanks. I thought I might have overdone it a bit for a place that serves steaks and burgers.' She let out a laugh that tinkled in my ears.

'I ordered beer for you.'

I stared at her, mesmerized by the kohl in her eyes.

'Johnny, why are you staring at me like that?'

'Am I?'

She blushed and replied, 'Reminds me of the theatre director, Mr Sarkar, "Oh, you poor hooker by the roadside" look.'

'Long-term patients can be really annoying. Don't worry, we'll get rid of Sarkar soon enough.'

'Johnny that reminds me, I did some reading on crystal meth and read up 203's chart. He's displaying none of the physical or behavioural effects of crystal meth anymore. I am not questioning your judgement, but in my professional opinion he's clean and ready to be shipped out.'

'Sera, I decide who comes in and who goes out. Trust me, it's for his own good to stay locked up.'

'We are not running a zoo and these are not animals. They are real people who get better in time and have a right to live a normal life like you and I.'

Her impassioned speech pushed all the wrong buttons. She must have sensed the change and fell silent. We stared at each other a long time, the silence no longer awkward, but an echo of our bodies waiting to be entwined. Somehow we got past the meal, the sexual tension making it impossible to have any real conversation.

It was eleven by the time we reached Thy Will and stood facing each other in the porch of the outhouse where Sera lived.

'Thanks, Sera, I had a great time.'

'So did I, Johnny.'

I traced her cheekbone with the tip of my finger, lingering on her lips. She stood still with stars in her eyes. I only had to bend my head a little to brush the moonlight on those moist lips, the glistening hollow between the collarbones, all the way down to the proud inviting peaks.

But I was hesitant to touch the innocence on that expectant face.

'Sweet dreams, Sera', was all I could manage. I didn't have the heart to tell her that the great Johnny Will was allergic to all things good and pure.

Journal of an Alcoholic

Mira is dead.

My sanity will die too. It is just a matter of time. A running journal keeps me sane. You see, the days are long and nights pitch-dark, and even though my memory plays tricks, I like to write. Just for a while, it makes me forget this deep-rooted sadness that refuses to leave, to leave me alone.

The hands that tremble in desolation,
The eyes that mirror desperation,
Belong to me,
Yet, I am a stranger to them,
The recognition is slow,
Several lifetimes I have fought,
This melancholy bravely . . . cowardly,
I must have,
A strong enemy such as this deep-rooted sadness,
Cannot be slain by a fragile mind.
The grave has been dug many times,
I have even said my prayers,
The tombstone reads,

'Here rest the damned,
The unloved, who haven't made their peace',
I laugh; God's great creation is a graveyard then,
Home to us immortals, wounded, hurt, afflicted,
The living-dead,
Not a hint of bravery, just an easy acceptance of this
deep-seated sadness.

I could have sworn it was Johnny there in her living room, kissing her lips as she lay on the settee, half-dead. I could have sworn it was Johnny. She was there too, or is she in my head, I can't be too sure. Adele has a way of messing up my mind.

God, someone help me, my head is beginning to spin.

The Clue

Monele had not an acre of land for sale. Everything that could be sold had been bought off over the years by swanky hotels and people setting up dream houses for their retirement. Privacy was of utmost importance to the gentry of Monele, hence most of the houses had high fences running around the property.

By some strange coincidence, I found myself standing outside the same complex from which Mira's body had been wheeled out.

The house across her building was a duplex and belonged to an ex-army top gun who had been reported missing by his wife. It wasn't my case; it was up to the local inspector to look into it. Petty thefts, threats and quarrels had been the only crimes in Monele for the last decade or so, until Mira's body was discovered.

So, it wasn't any surprise that this particular case had been gathering dust for two weeks till one afternoon, the concerned wife showed up at the police station where I happened to be.

'Inspector Nari, please, I beg you to find my husband,

something's happened, otherwise he would have contacted me. It's been two weeks.'

The elegant woman moved her hands desperately, looking from me to Nari, who seemed reluctant to leave the puffed idli he was about to bite into.

'Mrs Baines, there's not much we can do. We searched everywhere; maybe he's gone to the city. It does get lonely out here.'

The remark had angered Mrs Baines and she lashed out. 'He doesn't have any money. I told you that his wallet, his things are all at home. I mentioned it in the FIR, if you would only care to read!'

Nari's cheeks turned pink. He prepared to brush her off in the usual gruff 'police' manner, when I intervened.

'Tell me, Madame, when did you see your husband last?'

'On September the fourth, around eight p.m., he rushed out of the house in a great hurry and never came back.'

I sat up; it was the same evening Mira had died. 'I assume he didn't take the car?'

'No, he liked to walk.'

Her voice shook and I gave her a moment to recover.

'Is there anything else you can tell me? For instance, what was his behaviour like, who was the last person to see him besides you, things like that?'

'He . . . uh . . . was greatly upset after his weekly visit to the doctor's.'

'What is he being treated for?'

'He is, uh, rehabilitating from alcohol addiction. Dr Will had been treating him for the past few months.'

'I see! And you think Dr Will might have something to do with your husband's disappearance?'

'No, of course not, but alcoholics have little regard for people who are trying to treat them.'

She teared up, leant on the unstable bench nearby and sobbed. A little later, I found myself driving her home. It wasn't that Mrs Baines's tears affected me very much; I was intrigued by the involvement of Johnny Will.

My curiosity was rewarded: the general's house was in the same complex as Mira Kermani's. Things were beginning to get interesting.

I looked around the house while Mrs Baines repaired her face and made tea. I noticed they had separate bedrooms, hers was neat and his smelly and messy, so she clearly wasn't allowed in. Not a loving couple, I deduced.

There were medicines scattered everywhere, I picked up a couple to read the labels: Escitalopram, Lorazepam, seemingly harmless anti-anxiety and antidepressant pills.

Mrs Baines had not attempted to clean the place in her husband's absence, which spoke volumes about their strained relationship. His clothes were strewn all over the place, shirts, pyjamas, lungis. There was a pile of dusty files, containing bank statements, dividend sheets, income tax returns and other financial details. Many of them lay unopened, the general had not been fit enough to undertake the tedious task.

I turned over the stained bed cover and sheets; nothing there. Under the pile of pillows was a small transparent bottle with red capsules. Its label had the caricature of a bare-chested man stroking a long pointy moustache. The bottle looked like something sold on TV, like on Asian Sky Shop. I read the label and smiled; there was more to our general than met the eye. The capsules were for erectile dysfunction and upping the libido, which was not surprising considering the fact that a common side effect of alcoholism was sexual dysfunction. I put the bottle back. But something gnawed at me and I picked it up again. The bottle was nearly empty.

It didn't look like his wife was receiving any kind of attention at all. Who was the sixty-year-old retired general priming himself up for? Maybe he had run away with a woman several years younger than him.

The medicine had to be good if it had the general's ding-dong up and ticking. I read the label again, 'Sexanoil', committed it to memory and put it back. Who knows, it might come handy some day.

Smiling to myself, I peeped under the bed. Bottles of the finest malt stood there, mostly empty. Mrs Baines found me kneeling under the bed and coughed politely.

In my haste to get out from under the bed, I knocked a few bottles and they rolled in all directions. We both bent down to retrieve them and collected all except one that had rolled under the side table.

I stretched my hand as far as I could and fished the bottle out along with a red diary that had *Journal of an Alcoholic* embossed on it and a vulture perched on the insignia.

Many pages had been torn off and were missing and except for two lines on the first page, the rest of the diary was empty. I encouraged Mrs Baines to try and read the illegible handwriting of her husband of thirty years. She couldn't. In frustration, I tore the diary out of her hand, wore my glasses and strained to read the text.

Journal of an Alcoholic

I have no fear . . . perched on the ruins of fame,
A man crippled by shame.

There was a bit of a poet in me that recognized a fellow poet on the verge of a breakdown. This man had no intention of going on living; his writing was a cry for help. A declaration of failure, of surrender, I wondered then if he had already ended his life by jumping off a cliff. His dejection seemed to burn the pages of the red leather-bound journal.

The illusion of a suicide didn't last long. As I examined the journal more closely, it had the Thy Will emblem on one of the pages and the phone number of Dr Johnny Will. It seemed the expensive rehab centre provided an expensive leather diary to its patients to chart their thoughts out on paper. Having found the diary, I searched the room with a vengeance, found what I was looking for and put in a long-distance call.

'Sir, the general owns high-powered night-vision binoculars, that uh . . .'

'Ray, what's so irregular about an ex-army possessing a pair of binocs?' The commissioner's voice travelled well into Mrs Baines living room.

'Sir, even as I speak I am looking into Mira Kermani's living room, a very clear view of the place where she was found dead.'

'Good! Then bring in the general for questioning and stop harassing Dr Will.'

The commissioner was a fairly likeable man, but in moments like these it became difficult to ignore that his brain had long ceased to function like a policeman's. I had just told him that the general had gone missing the same evening that the Kermani girl had died. Jackass.

'Sir, it's a long shot, but the same man might be responsible for the general's disappearance, considering that Monele is such a peaceful town.'

'The drunkard must have fallen into a ditch or something.'

'Nothing has been reported so far, sir,' I persisted.

'What reason would a dignified ex-army officer have for spying on Mira Kermani?'

An image of the bottle of Sexanoil flashed in my mind.

'Uh, I'll let you know as soon as I figure that part, sir. Goodnight.'

I disconnected the phone before he could raise further objections, and went in search of Mrs Baines to thank her for the tea and assure her that I would find her husband in the next twenty-four hours.

'Did you see the general on the fourth of September around six p.m.?'

'Can't say, must have,' said Adele Will, nonchalantly.

'Mrs Baines says the general was a regular at Café Aspen.'

'Men like to get away from their nagging wives at least once a day.'

'Yes, but no matter where they might be taking their coffee, most men return home when the sun goes down. This one didn't; any idea why?'

'Don't know, don't care. He was just another customer.'

'Not good enough. That was the last evening that you saw him, come on refresh your memory.'

'He said he was going to the rehab to pick up his medication, or at least that's what he told me. You should probably ask my nephew what he did with the general.'

She smiled and disappeared inside. The general had disappeared the night of Mira's death and his house was right across from hers. There was a connection there. I was sure Adele knew more, but I had no way of getting it out of her. Johnny's involvement in both the cases seemed certain now. I wasn't going to let him get away this time, and the only way to catch Johnny was to catch him with his hand in the cookie jar.

SERA

Head in the Mud

Not even a peck on the cheek! That, in my books, is the definition of a disastrous date. Even my husband (as good as dead to me now) had once inspired feelings of such great passion that at twenty-one, marrying a forty-six-year-old man had seemed like a dream come true.

Yet, my heart never pined for him as it pined for Johnny. All evening I had waited for the goodnight kiss that never came. Yet, I could have sworn that Johnny was close to kissing me . . .

At twenty-nine, I was behaving like a schoolgirl with a first crush, for here I was, lurking in the compound, hoping to bump into Johnny.

As I walked through the enclosed yard that allows patients to enjoy fresh air and a glimpse of the sky, I noticed patient 203 carving out something on the wooden bench.

'You have to give me that nail. I can't have you damage the property of the facility.' I bent to pull it out of his hand gently, but he resisted and caught my wrist in a steel grip.

'Are you sure it's the destruction of private property you are worried about, Doc?'

The wind was blowing his shaggy, shoulder-length hair as he assessed my face. I grew self-conscious as he continued to stare. I had handled many difficult patients, young, old, jerks, gentlemen, but no one with his movie star looks and persona. Handcuffed, in a dirty white jumpsuit and a heavy beard, he still radiated charisma.

'You need to hand it over, or I'll have to summon the orderlies and cut short your relaxation time.'

'Relaxation time!' He started to laugh loudly and other patients looked our way.

'Think it's a picnic, Doc, to be let out in the yard like some dangerous animal in handcuffs?'

I had never known Johnny to restrain any other patient, sane patient, like this. 'You must have done something to deserve this.'

He jumped up and brought the nail close, barely inches away from my left eye. My heart skipped a beat. I wanted to call for help, but pride in my professional capacity wouldn't let me give in to his terror tactics. I gave a nervous laugh, in an attempt at fake confidence, and said, 'I am sorry; it came out a little rude, you seem like a nice person.'

That made him smile and he dropped the rusted nail in the palm of my free hand. I breathed a very audible sigh of relief and he whispered in my ears, 'Scared?'

So engaging was his manner that I was letting this mad man in handcuffs chat me up.

'A little.'

'Sorry, it's been a while that I have been around a beautiful woman.'

'What did you do before you . . .'

'Got locked away? I am an artist, I paint, I sculpt, did a

couple of exhibitions in London. A promising debut, I believe was the verdict. I am not as young and worthless as I look.'

I was impressed. He couldn't have been a day older than twenty-one.

'Is your art . . . shocking?' I asked.

'Occupational hazard, art needs to be scandalous enough to shock audiences into a reaction.' Suddenly his body stiffened and he stood up. 'Run little lamb, the wolf is on the prowl.'

Before I could comprehend it, Johnny stood over us. He gave me a chilling look that gave me goosebumps. He turned to address patient 203.

'Up to your monkey tricks, huh?'

'Your staff is very helpful. The doc here has pretty manners, unlike you.'

'Not pretty enough to be your muse.'

The last remark dented my vanity in a big way.

Sunny, the head orderly, was summoned and he whisked 203 to his room.

'Stay away from him, Sera. You are a goddamn doctor, not a silly schoolgirl.' Johnny looked pointedly at the front of my tee that read, 'love me'.

'He is far more civilized than you, with all your fancy degrees and haughty manners!' I was in the mood to let off some steam.

'Sure, he spits out foolish women like you for breakfast.'

'How dare you speak to me like this? I was just doing my job!'

'Which, I clearly remember telling you, is to stay away from that psychopath.'

'Who is he, why is he so important to you, Johnny?'

'He's a murderer. The next time I find you speaking to him will be your last day at Thy Will.'

He spoke with such vehemence that I was tongue-tied. I didn't know what to think anymore. Did he or did he not feel something for me? I sank into the wooden bench that Prince Charming had occupied a while ago.

My hand inadvertently grazed over the freshly carved name on the bench and I turned to look at what was written.

Mira.

She was everywhere; her death had made her larger than life. Even the madman seemed to have a strong connection with her. A wooden splinter pricked my finger and blood oozed out. With determined strides I marched down the corridor to room 203. He had been sedated and was on the verge of drifting into the safe haven of sleep, when I called out through the steel bars, 'How do you know Mira?'

He opened his eyes and sang in his drunken state;

'Johnny had a little rabbit,
Mira had a fucking habit,
Rabbit died, Mira lied, Johnny cried!'

The third Saturday of the month was scheduled for group therapy, something on the lines of Alcoholic Anonymous. Sobered-up alcoholics recounted their struggle to remain upbeat, the nightly seduction by alcohol, the temptress, their dwindling self-worth, failing personal and professional equations.

Since the inception of Thy Will, these sessions had been

facilitated by Johnny, but my growing competence had forced him to acknowledge the fact that it was time I was given a chance to prove myself.

Having conducted three successful sessions so far, I was starting to get confident. Johnny still came towards the end to give a short but mesmerizing speech that always brought grudging smiles to the tired, haggard faces.

The numbers could never be anticipated as they came when they could; the session is open to all: patients, ex-patients, non-patients. The popularity of this monthly meeting had grown.

Today, I faced a group of eleven. They didn't need any prompting to get on with their stories, so I sat back and stared into space, reflecting upon my sad existence, kicking myself for loving a man who was cold as an iceberg. Even if he didn't think I was pretty enough for his taste, he didn't have to actually say it out loud.

Adding insult to injury was the madman's tribute to Mira, carved on the wooden bench. Was I so insignificant in front of that dead woman, that living, breathing men wouldn't spare me a glance? And what was I to make of the twisted rhyme stuck in my mind? Did Johnny even have a rabbit? What had Mira been lying about? How did 203 even know these things? There was so much I didn't know. The only way to get some answers was to get Marie to talk. But how to pry loose her tongue?

'The golden silence!'

Johnny's voice boomed from behind me, so lost was I that it didn't register that the group had fallen silent. I looked around to find boredom, agitation and even resentment in their mannerism. As a facilitator, I was supposed to encourage individuals to open up and answer their questions, clear any doubts but I did none of that. I was about to apologize, but Johnny quelled it with a look loaded with displeasure and addressed his audience.

'What do my wife or husband, children, parents know of my troubles, the pressures of life, of earning a living, of competition, of failure, of love, of lust, of hurt, of death?'

There was a collective 'hmmm' from the group.

Johnny smiled. 'But you can't wash the unpleasantness down with a peg of whisky, can you? Neither is life's meaning at the bottom of a bottle nor the solution of your life-threatening problems. Stand up and look your fears in the face, you are your only ally at this point. No one can help you but you.'

Twenty minutes later, they all left, after helping themselves to the refreshments laid out on the table, more charged up than when they had come in. Once again, Johnny and I stood facing each other. I wanted to say many things but the words could not move past the lump in my throat. My hands shook as I handed him a Styrofoam cup of coffee. He leant against the table and offered me a marble cake.

'Johnny, are you going to pull me off the group session?'

'Are you telling me you can't handle the pressure anymore, the whining note in their voice, the suffering in their eyes?'

His sarcasm was making me angry. 'I am saying no such thing. I can handle this!'

'Swell! Just don't go all blank on our rich suckers. They come here to be heard and not to endure the painful silence of your company.'

'Why are you being so rude to me lately?'

Johnny didn't think the question deserved an answer. He calmly put his coffee aside, flashed a smile reserved for clingy pets and turned to go. If it were possible to choke on anger, I would have.

'Go hide, lick your wounds and live your pathetic life all by yourself,' I hurled at his retreating back.

He stopped in his tracks and walked all the way to where I was standing, shaking. 'Saying those things made you happy, Sera?'

'Don't you dare psychoanalyse me!'

'I won't. Now stop crying, sweetheart.'

Then it happened, just like that, he leant forward and kissed the teardrop trickling down my cheek. I stared in confusion as his hands held me lightly. Again, he ignored the blatant invitation on my lips, and instead whispered in my ears, 'Be strong, Sera, you have to look after Thy Will in my absence.'

'Johnny, can I not come with you?' I whispered back.

'I hope not.'

Even as my brain struggled to make sense of it all, another sound caught my attention; a car skidding on the gravel in our driveway and the furious barking of dogs. Seconds later, an entourage of uniformed policemen and two ferocious German shepherds barged in and a senior-looking officer waved a paper in front of our eyes.

'Dr Johnny Will, we have a search warrant for your house, the premises and everything in between.'

'May I ask what you are looking for, Officer Ray?' Johnny asked calmly.

'Just about anything I can nail you with.'

There was a sharp intake of breath and belatedly I realized it was me.

Officer Ray turned his attention to me and said, 'I believe we haven't met before. I am Officer Ray, Sera.'

He mentioned my name casually, as if to let me know that he had done his homework. It remained to be seen how much he actually knew and how much of it was routine information.

The officers began their search and Johnny was made to sit in his cabin with a policeman guarding his door. They ransacked the files, the drawers and the décor like petty thieves. Johnny's orderly life was torn to bits as he sat brooding in his glasshouse. For some reason, Officer Ray asked me to accompany him on his walk through the premises.

His men rounded up all the patients in the yard, while a search of their rooms was carried out.

One room in particular caught Officer Ray's attention. It made me wonder if he knew who the previous occupant of the room was. It had been swept clean after the general's discharge almost a month ago and was unoccupied. However, nothing useful was revealed and we moved on to the next room, room 203, the most unkempt room in the facility; footmarks adorned the wall where 203 practised his kicks.

'Whose room is this?'

'Sorry, doctor–patient confidentiality.'

He didn't pursue it any further. What was I supposed to tell him anyway? That I had no clue who the good-looking madman was?

They carried on relentlessly, hour after hour, not in the least bit disappointed at not finding anything. Maybe the whole idea behind the search was to intimidate Johnny? It would take a whole lot more to intimidate my Johnny. My Johnny, that's how I thought of him now, as mine.

The sun was about to set when Officer Ray decided to do a preliminary search of the lawn and the acres of land that had been converted into a kitchen garden.

The sniffer dogs followed a trail, sniffing, shaking their heads, pulling their handlers in the direction of the garden. They seemed puzzled and kept running from a pile of manure to freshly dug-out field prepared for planting winter vegetables. These fields catered to the entire vegetable requirement of Thy Will round the year, and were part of the de-stressing activities chalked out for inpatients, under supervision of course.

The more the dogs sniffed, the more excited they became. Officer Ray asked the handlers to let them off the leash. I was petrified and stood rooted to the spot as the ferocious animals ran past me and lunged at the mini mountain of manure and began digging furiously.

There was a growing sense of urgency all around. Within minutes, the manure pile had been razed to the ground. Officer Ray leant forward, looked back, disappointment written all over his face. I told Officer Ray that I was getting myself a cup of tea.

Tea never happened; the stench from the freshly dug ground was so putrid that everyone held their breath. Shovels were quickly brought out and the source of the smell was unearthed. The general's shrivelled-up body was covered in dried blood. There were maggots crawling through the crevices in his abdomen; he had been stabbed many times. What was even more horrifying was that his head had been severed from his neck. I shrank away from the revolting sight, not knowing whether to run or to stay. For Johnny, my Johnny's sake, I had to brave it out.

The body was lifted sans the head and something shiny caught the last light of the evening – a 20-ml syringe! A syringe big enough to hold a lethal dose that could kill.

Officer Ray slipped on white plastic gloves, and with a tweezer in his hand, knelt next to the body. He pushed aside a wisp of hair from the general's face, exposing the terrified look on his face as worms crawled out of his open eyes and nose. Officer Ray mumbled a prayer.

I wanted to pray too, but the numbness in my heart had made my limbs cold. The general's horrifying end did not affect me much; my thoughts were on Johnny. Officer Ray, it turned out, was more sensitive to the general's death than I.

'A grave with no headstone, no flowers, no footnote, is a grave made in haste, in very poor taste,' said Officer Ray, solemnly.

A Run-in with the Law

They had found something. I could hear the commotion in the backyard. Slowly, through the glass doors. I wondered what it was and the feeling of doom returned. I picked up the phone and called Zac.

'I want you to pick up all the tapes filed under patient information from the record room and put them someplace safe.'

'Why are you worried, Johnny? Those tapes have nothing to do with the murder investigation.'

'You and I know the tapes are harmless, the police don't. The next thing we know they'll charge us with blackmailing patients. They'll do anything to make it stick.'

Travelling in the back of a shabby Jeep is a novel experience. The journey to Ooty lasted the better part of an hour in which I was told nothing. Officer Ray did not accompany us, but I knew instinctively that whatever they had found in the backyard was damaging enough to have made my arrest possible.

I prayed that Zac got to the tapes before Ray decided to add abuse of doctor–patient privilege to my list of crimes.

Sera's sweet, innocent face popped up before my eyes. She was right; my pathetic life desperately needed a woman's reassurance. The passion in a woman's eyes alone could uplift the waning spirits of a man in my dire straits, accused of, and now probably arrested for, murder.

The Jeep stopped outside the police station and I was escorted to a room with a table and a chair that had been repaired too many times. The criminal chat room had no other amenities to offer. I sat down and closed my eyes; there were some decisions to be made. Ray showed up an hour later.

'Where's the murder weapon, Johnny?'

'Didn't you find it in my backyard, Ray?'

'You can't talk yourself out of this mess.'

'Alright, then, get me a lawyer and at least tell me on what basis I have been arrested.'

'Okay, if that's the way you want to play it. Surprise, surprise! We found the general's body dumped under a pile of manure!'

'What? Why did he have to die in my backyard?'

'Probably because he saw you through his binoculars from his window, injecting Mira with morphine; he had to be silenced.'

'That's ridiculous.'

'Well, to dump the syringe along with the body under the manure pile must have seemed like an ingenuous idea at that time.'

I kept quiet. The silence stretched. It's an old trick to make the other party talk. I am the psychiatrist, I know these mind games. He was the first to break the silence, after twenty dragging minutes.

'A 20-ml syringe and a butcher's knife seemed to have done the trick. Want to confess how you severed his head from his neck?'

'Fuck!' I couldn't stop myself from cursing. 'I had nothing to do with him! And just because you found his body in my garden doesn't mean I killed him. There are about twenty people working at Thy Will, other than my nutcase inpatients and outpatients.'

'Oh, the killer's out there while I am wasting my time grilling a nobody?'

'Ray, I think Mira was seeing someone. That someone killed her, not me.'

'Hah! The reputation of a pregnant girl is of little consequence now that she's dead.'

'Do a DNA test.'

'Well, if the baby is not yours then you probably killed her, Johnny. I'll bet my last rupee on it.'

'You never asked if the child was mine, you just assumed it was.'

'I did.'

With that Ray stepped out and I was left in the dark to fight the ugly thoughts that grew in my mind. Did my patients feel the same helplessness at being locked up against their wishes, with no one to talk to? Did a locked room do more damage than good? Was fate teaching me a lesson for playing by my rules? Overcome by fatigue I dozed off and woke up to find Ray standing on my head, bellowing my name.

Johnny, wake up! Time to go home.'

'Home?'

'Yes, home on bail, rich boy. It's hard to keep a man who plays golf with the district magistrate behind bars over the weekend. Particularly when the influential father of the murdered girl decides to rescue her lover.'

'Kermani bailed me out? Swell!'

'You watch out, Johnny.'

'Thanks for the heads-up. Can I leave now?'

'Not so fast, I'll need some samples for the paternity test. You are not going to back out now, are you?'

'Happy to help.'

Sera was waiting outside for me. I got in the car and started the engine without looking at her.

'Who asked you to come?'

'No one, this good deed is solely my idea.'

We drove in silence. The road from Ooty to Monele was fine, but the absence of streetlights made the bends extra-tricky. Today, though, I couldn't care less and drove like a madman. I could tell Sera was scared, but she didn't utter a word of admonishment. After a while, my anger subsided and I apologized to her – a mistake, because she now thought I was willing to make conversation.

'Kermani must really like you to have posted bail. I knew he's rich and powerful but I didn't know how powerful until now.'

'Oh, you would be surprised at what people are willing to do for their loved ones.'

'I didn't know you shared that kind of a relationship with Mira's father.'

'I was allowed one phone call from the jail to call my lawyer and I chose to call Kermani instead; it worked.'

'Why Kermani of all people?'

'I have something he needs.'

'God! Please tell me you are not blackmailing him.'

The whole thing sounded so funny that I burst out laughing.

'No, stupid girl. I have been babysitting his nephew for a while and it is time I called in a few favours.'

'Patient 203?'

'Yup, the one and only. Azaan Kermani is Mira's first cousin and now the scion of Kermani's empire.'

'He must love Mira very much.'

'You are right, Sera, he did. Did you know that among Parsis it's fucking common for first cousins to marry?'

'I meant her father, Johnny.'

I knew Kaizad Kermani well enough through the eyes of his precious daughter. Mira shared with him a rare bond of love and respect. Many a late night, her head on my chest, she would recount quirky tales of her childhood spent with her father. She once told me how her father had saved a man from being eaten by a crocodile. He had bravely jumped into the lake to rescue a local whose boat had capsized. The crocodile had waded into the water from the other end, but Kermani out swam the reptile by dragging the man out in time. A heroic tale that had made me angry. I had no taste for such stories. My own father had never shown any bravery, he had not even been outdoors or seen the sunlight in the last few years of his life. I hated listening to her happy childhood tales, but I couldn't tell her to get out of bed just after I had made love to her. I suffered through the stories. All of those tales about her father and the family's history came back to me now.

It had taken Kermani twenty years to get acceptance from thc local community. They would call him the mad man from Bombay who had come to sell Parsi delicacies to the village folk. In time, the Parsis had grown in number and started running small inns around town.

But none of them tasted success as Kermani, who turned a bistro into a palatial resort. The local staff was the recipient of his generosity and his goodwill grew.

Yet, strange are the quirks of fate. The man who had built so much had no one to bequeath his heritage. His daughter was dead and the only surviving nephew was a fucking addict.

To the Rescue

Getting Johnny out on bail was easy enough. God forbid, if a body is found in the Seven Seas, those idiots will just walk in and handcuff me because the property belongs to me. It's the same argument I gave the district magistrate and a personal guarantee that Johnny couldn't be involved in Mira's or the general's death.

A bunch of idiots run the police force and Officer Ray seems more of a nuisance now. The heat is settling down, and Mira's death is no longer the topic of conversation at every club in town. I had raised her as a son and that's probably where I went wrong. A daughter, no matter how tough and resilient, will always remain a cause of worry for her old man. I miss her.

It was time to bring Azaan out. He wasn't present at Mira's funeral. He'll never say it, but I know he'll nurse that grudge against me for the rest of his life.

I no longer cared for Johnny's professional opinion about the need to monitor Azaan constantly. What he needed was to keep his mind occupied before it rotted away in that cell. Azaan had to see beyond his nude paintings and drugs. I had so much more to offer. Mira was gone, but the show at the Seven Seas must go on, and Azaan was going to run it for me.

I called my PA and asked him to cancel my schedule for the rest of the day. It was time I paid a visit to Thy Will.

The old house had recently been painted white. The lawn was well maintained, its roses in full bloom. An imposing banyan tree partially barred the foyer. The two-storeyed house must have had over a dozen rooms, not counting the large halls, study room, children's nursery and attic.

Mira loved Thy Will and had explored it at leisure. She wanted to replicate it at the Seven Seas. I had made a vague promise and had forgotten about it until today.

I imagined Mira in the very house I now stood in, whose owner had loved her enough to have asked her to marry him last summer. Mira loved Johnny in her own way, but marrying him was never an option. Azaan was always the first preference.

I hovered around the banyan in a bid to spot somebody who could guide me to Johnny; a young girl with strikingly dark hair and a pair of unusually curious eyes stopped by me.

'May I help you?

'I wish to see Dr Will.'

'You do have an appointment, sir?'

'Afraid not, young lady, just tell him Mira's father is here to see him.'

Her jaw dropped, in a manner of speaking, and she hurried to convey the message to her employer. The back of her T-shirt read, 'Ride me.'

I wonder what Mira would have made of that suggestive tee. Minutes later, I was reclining in Johnny's cabin.

'Mr Kermani, I can't thank you enough for rescuing me from that hellhole.'

'Don't mention it. Mira would have wanted me to.'

Mira's name dulled the light in Johnny's eyes. 'What brings you here, Mr Kermani?'

'I wanted to review Azaan's progress . . .'

'We could have done it over the phone.'

'I want to take him home. He's been here nine months now, surely he's cured?'

'Have you read any of the notes that I sent you over the last few months?'

'Johnny, I don't understand the medical mumbo-jumbo. Once you take the drugs out of my boy's system, he's as good as new. You have done that successfully before, then why is he still here?'

'He's given to violent fits of rage, Mr Kermani, and they have nothing to do with drugs.' Johnny paused. 'Azaan suffers from Intermittent Explosive Disorder, a behavioural disorder characterized by extreme expressions of anger, often to the point of uncontrollable rage, that are disproportionate to the situation at hand. IED is usually a sign that bipolar disorder is around the corner.'

'I have raised him as a son for twenty long years and know that he's not capable of hurting an insect, let alone a person.'

Johnny continued in his clear voice, as if he was reading an excerpt from a book. 'Bipolar disorder is a psychiatric diagnosis that describes a category of mood disorders. Azaan experiences manic episodes and depression that occur in a cyclic pattern. Maybe that's what happened when Azaan attacked the girl in his college in London.'

'Azaan was there with ten other people, anyone of them could have done it, they were all piss drunk. My boy is not crazy as you suggest. He comes from the finest blood!'

'It doesn't have to be genetic. There is significant evidence to suggest that many people with creative talents suffer from some form of bipolar disorder.'

'I don't care what you say. I am here to take him with me.'

Johnny picked up the phone and gave the orders. Ten minutes later, Azaan, escorted by the young woman whom Johnny addressed as Sera, came in and we hugged each other.

'The beard suits you, Tiger!'

'They refused to give me a blade to shave, for fear I would slit my throat – or maybe someone else's!' he said, radiating humour and good health.

'That's nonsense, we are going home!'

The discharge formalities took some time, and with each passing minute, Azaan grew restless, tapping his foot, drumming his fingers and whistling an old country tune, oblivious to his surroundings. I noticed his eyes resting on Sera every time she came around. That Azaan had plans for Sera was obvious as a wart on the face. I felt a little uneasy. What if Johnny was right and Azaan needed more time at Thy Will? I came to a decision.

'Johnny, as discussed, Azaan will be continuing therapy and will be here for his bi-monthly sessions as and when you can accommodate him.'

There was silence in the room. Johnny cleared his throat and said, 'Excellent idea, Mr Kermani.'

I could not gauge Azaan's reaction; there wasn't any. He continued whistling and stopped only to say, 'Be seeing you, Doc.'

Before Johnny could think of a suitable reply, Azaan winked at Sera and walked out of the room.

Lady Baines

The Widow

I was grateful to God that my children were not here when the news came. I couldn't have borne the look of disdain in their eyes. His body had lain on the cold morgue slab, skilfully stitched together to hide the stab wounds. Not much could be done about the head.

Thirty-five years of togetherness went up in flames along with my husband's body. The funeral was a quick, shabby affair.

My son and daughter had rushed home without their families – my grandchildren had school that they couldn't miss to attend grandpa's funeral. I couldn't stop the tears that ran down my face, thinking about what an appalling end this brave soldier had met with. The alcohol had destroyed the respect and name it had taken him years to earn.

Still, many people had turned up for the funeral. The news of the murder had attracted quite a crowd.

Dr Will stood in one corner, staring at the pyre while his pretty assistant kept glancing at him from the corner of her eye.

The general had never liked Dr Will, but I knew he had a grudging admiration for the cause he stood for. In the last few years, I had seen the helplessness in my husband's eyes. There were nights when he didn't want to drink, but his body craved the poison, the pain unbearable, and surrender came far too easy. I got pushed further and further into the background, sari-clad, a string of pearls around the neck, keeping up the pretence that all was well with the Baines.

Every night, my teenage children would witness the screaming matches and the drunken drama. Their confusion in time turned into resentment and each one left as soon as he or she could. Despite the general's addiction, he was a generous father who took great pride in the achievements of his children and gave them every possible opportunity to spread their wings. Today, my children were as alien to me as the husband who left me without so much as a loving word.

The stigma of a failed marriage kept me from admitting that there was a problem. By the time reality set in, there was no place to turn to; my parents were long dead, I had left a career in teaching in favour of a family life, and the fear of being alone paralysed me. So here I was, a widow of fifty-seven with no financial worries, a huge bungalow and little to look forward to.

I wonder if things would have turned out differently for me and my children if I had walked out on him on that fateful Sunday afternoon seventeen years ago. Well, now there was enough time to ponder upon regrets and missed opportunities.

I turned to greet Dr Will.

'I am deeply sorry for your loss, Mrs Baines.'

A wan smile was all I could muster; he had, after all, been

taken into custody for my husband's death. There was an uncomfortable silence all around; we were under the scrutiny of every person present at the funeral.

'If there's anything I can do, Mrs Baines . . .' his voice trailed off.

He took his leave and joined his assistant. Together, they looked beautiful in the winter sunshine, young and in love, as the general and I had been once. Maybe life would be kinder to them than it had been to us.

The general was a Lovedale alumnus, and many of his friends from school had turned up for the funeral. I knew some by face, others by name and some not at all. Formal introductions were made, condolences expressed and then they too were on their way.

Hands folded, I bid each one farewell, including my grown-up children with busy careers and pre-scheduled flights. They left after extending hurried invitations to visit them after I had wrapped up the estate. There wasn't much to do; he had willed everything to me and to our children after me.

I stared at their retreating backs, holding back tears that threatened to mar the dignified image I presented.

Even the sun had been overpowered by the taunting dark clouds, as if telling me that my bleak existence had become bleaker. Kneeling by the pyre, a sudden gust of loneliness came over me, and my reserve of twenty years dissolved.

I cursed the general for abandoning me. 'What have I to live for? Our children don't need me, something else they picked up from you. Do you hear me?' I was shouting, but I couldn't stop myself. 'My life has been a lie! A lie I lived for thirty-five long years; bearing the shame and the loneliness while you drank our lives away. A lie, do you hear me?'

Strong arms lifted me from the ground and helped me stand. Officer Ray whispered in a quiet voice:

'I lie, I lie very often,
Sometimes I don't even remember,
At times I don't wish to,
Still, I like my memories clean,
They may not be worth a dime,
But they are all I have,
The ashes in the urn,
To hold tight, on a dark, lonely night.'

I hastily brushed the tears away and willed myself to smile to assure him that I could now be trusted with my own company. He made no move to leave; in silence, we took the narrow path that led to my bungalow. I could sense he had something on his mind and urged him to share it with me.

'You know of any friends the general might have had during his stay at Thy Will?'

'None that I know of.'

'How did he spend his day?'

'As I told you earlier, he read the newspaper, did some odd jobs around the house, noon was gin and soda, after a light lunch he liked to nap. He spent his evening at the café, drinking coffee, chatting up with other retirees.'

'What about his equation with the owner of the café, Adele Will? Were they friendly?'

'Like all army officers, he was courteous, flirtatious, nothing more to it.'

'But he went there every day?'

'Officer Ray, whatever may be my husband's faults, womanizing wasn't one of them.'

The look on his face said he didn't believe me. I had lost my taste for company and conversation. I simply wanted him to leave so that I could be alone with my misery.

'Thank you, Officer Ray, for doing your duty. Most people would dismiss it as a drunk falling in a ditch and getting himself killed.'

'Mrs Baines, please call me if you remember anything out of the ordinary, a letter, a phone call. Anything at all.'

'I did receive a strange phone call a few weeks ago on the general's birthday; the man left a strange message, something about 203 calling. He spoke like the Bond fellow in the movies.'

'He had an accent?'

'Yes.'

'What was the general's reaction when you relayed the message to him?'

'He had laughed loudly and said, "son of a bitch".'

Sera

Kiss Me Tender

The evenings were getting nippy. I didn't particularly enjoy this time of year, when the sun set early and everyone went indoors to enjoy an early supper with their families. I had none. What I did have was a very comfortable accommodation, one of the perks of working for a wealthy man.

I shared the outhouse with Marie; it was equipped with a kitchenette, but Marie preferred to carry our meals in from the main house.

The last four years had just zipped by. Marie had been curious in the early days about why a decent-looking young woman would want to spend her life playing nurse to crazy patients. Over many long, cold evenings by the fire, I had tried to explain to her that I enjoyed the solitude. The explanation sounded feeble to my own ears, but after a while Marie had let it go and we had quickly settled into a routine chat every night over dinner.

There were still fifteen minutes before Marie rang the dinner bell. From my window, I could see the light in Johnny's study. My heart beat like a schoolgirl's at the thought of him sitting in his rocking chair, sipping wine, reading a medical journal and smoking a cigar.

I would often drop in to discuss something earlier, but had stopped when Mira started frequenting Thy Will.

It had been difficult at first to accept that he was as attracted to her as she was to him. Her laughter would echo down the corridor, halting all those who sought Johnny's attention.

In those moments, I had hated her for being rich, beautiful and single, everything that I was not. She had Marie eating out of her hands in less than a week, but she hardly ever spared me a glance.

I had once overheard her telling Johnny, 'She looks traumatized with so many patients in your waiting room.'

'She'll manage fine, Mira,' he had said.

'It's your practice at stake, not mine.'

I didn't wait to hear what Johnny had to say, pouring all my energy into work instead. Their love had grown, so had my professional competence, and with it, my confidence.

I was not the meek, insecure girl of twenty-five anymore. I knew exactly what I wanted from life and I was going after it now that the circumstances seemed favourable.

How difficult could it be to make someone love you is a question I ask myself often. The answer was always the same: 'you would never know if you didn't try'. I decided to have a candid chat with Marie without raising her hackles.

The dead body in the garden, police in the house and Johnny's trip to the police station had taken its toll. She was even more tight-lipped than ever.

'Who could have hidden the general's body in the garden?'

'May his soul rest in peace, let's not discuss unpleasant things at the dinner table, Sera.'

'Don't you ever think about it, Marie? It's got to be someone working here.'

'All I know is my Johnny didn't do it; that's all I care for!'

We ate in silence for a while. I didn't want to push my luck with Marie and waited for her to speak.

'I feel for him, Sera! He's been on his own since Daisy died. His father was a good-for-nothing bloke. And coming into so much money at such an early age gave Johnny ideas that maybe he could give back to the world what had been taken from him.'

'Maybe Zac and Aunt Adele staying here would have made a difference?'

'Adele is the devil in a female form, I tell you, a disgrace to us women folk! I remember the day they had bought Johnny in, half-dead, blood spewing everywhere. The she-devil had stood over him, cold as a fish, checking his pulse to see if he was dead or alive and had very calmly ordered me, "Marie, get someone to drive us to the hospital."'

'Johnny had been in an accident then?'

'Yes, a terrible accident, can we not talk about it on the dinner table, my child, it upsets my digestion.'

I mustered up courage and asked the question that was uppermost in my mind. 'Marie, do you think Johnny will ever get over her?'

Her penetrating eyes took in the faint colour that had come into my cheeks before she replied, 'I don't know, child. Despite the horrid things people say about my Johnny, I have never known him to give up on anyone – living or dead. But time is a great healer and so is a woman's touch.'

With these last words she gave me an enigmatic smile in the direction of the light coming from Johnny's study and rose from the table to clear up after dinner.

That's all I needed. I changed out of my dowdy nightdress and walked up to his study. The first knock went unheard. Knocking boldly the second time, I didn't wait to be invited in. A wise man had once said, 'It always pays to make an entry.'

I did, only to find him listening to country music with his eyes closed and a goblet full of red wine for company. The resting face of a loved one is a delight to watch.

I felt the adoration wash over me and I could not stop my hand from brushing the hair off his face. He did not open his eyes, but the corner of his mouth twitched.

That cynical smile sent me scurrying to the door when he called out: 'Stay.'

'It's me – Sera,' I said foolishly.

'I know.'

'How?'

'Your perfume.'

'I don't wear any.'

He opened his eyes lazily and said, 'Must be the scent of your pheromones in overdrive.'

For a minute, I was appalled that Johnny should speak to me like that, but the mischief lurking in his eyes made me smile.

'Is it heady, the scent?'

'Intoxicating.' He let out a deep breath to make a point and stood up to refill his own goblet and offer one to me.

In companionable silence, we sat listening to Sinatra's '*Strangers in the night*'.

'You know, Sera, by some strange coincidence, each line echoes the thought in my mind. Care to hear it again?'

He played the song again, and I couldn't help wondering

to myself, what were our chances? Was love a warm, embracing glance away?

This must have brought a smile to my face because the next thing I knew was that Johnny's eyes were staring deep into mine.

'Why did you come?'

A thousand lies came to my mind, but I told the truth. 'To be with you.'

'I may not be around for long.' He smiled.

It made me want to throw my arms around him. Seconds later, Johnny pulled me into his arms and held me close. Feelings I have never experienced before rose up in waves as I snuggled close. I remembered a time when Father had stroked my hair in a similar manner, murmuring endearments, making promises that a child of five could not comprehend.

I wasn't a child anymore. I knew the stakes.

Johnny was lonely, hurting and in need of affection. This did not necessarily translate into the happily-ever-after I so desperately wanted for myself.

Fearing that my gamble might not pay off, I gently tried to pull back.

'Running away?'

'Yes.'

'We are halfway through. Don't you want to know what's on the other side?'

'Heartbreak, probably.'

'And if I promise not to break your heart?'

It was my turn to smile and throw caution to the wind. 'You will, but you may kiss me anyway.'

As soon as the words were out, his lips found mine, tugging gently, teasing, as he found his way in. My body felt like putty in his hands, but he sought passion not surrender. In my limited experience, I had never known that a man could so match his rhythm to mine. There are the quintessential taking types and the pleasing kinds, but this was a man who wanted me to kiss him back.

So I kissed as I had never kissed before. If it were possible for a human form to melt into another, it was now. Somehow we landed on the couch, his body pressed against mine. I longed to be touched, devoured. Johnny felt it too, the burning need to merge, yet he held back.

Probably, the significance of our transition from the professional to the intimate was sinking in. He stroked my midriff lazily.

His eyes were a pool of dark, swirling passion. A warning jangled in my head – it was a flame of possession, not tenderness that inflamed his face. There was a connection here, I could feel it in my bones that destiny had plans for both of us, not necessarily grand!

But the real question was, did he? Could he see beyond his love for Mira; was I just a passing attraction?

He kissed me again and wiped my chin clean with a swift movement of his tongue. A vague sound in the background took his attention away from me. He placed a finger on my lips and we stayed like that for a while.

It was difficult to interpret the calculating look on his face as he disengaged himself and calmly went to the door and yanked it open. Zac stood on the other side, looking not in the least bit guilty. With a sheepish grin, he walked in.

'Quite a gathering! Hello, Sera.'

Too preoccupied with smoothening my hair, I gave him half a smile. The awkward moment was diffused by Johnny, who shoved a wine glass under Zac's nose.

'Thanks. It's been a tiring day for me. We need to find Mira's replacement.' His glance fell my way. 'I mean professionally.'

I wondered if Zac had an agenda. Why would he deliberately go on talking about Mira. Zac was nobody's fool and the tension in the room was hard to miss.

I had mixed feelings about him. He was always courteous and correct, but something in his manner towards Johnny didn't ring true. There was no visible strain in their relationship, yet they didn't sit down like ordinary cousins and share a meal or make small talk.

Zac came in every day as any other employee at Thy Will, punched himself in and went about his work. The recent discovery that he was keeping tabs on errant patients did not endear him much to me.

'Have the test results come?'

Johnny's clipped 'no' piqued my curiosity and I asked, 'What results?'

They both looked at me as though they had forgotten I was still in the room. I repeated the question.

'The paternity test results to see whether the baby in Mira's womb was mine.'

The news hit me hard. I felt tears swimming in my eyes. Zac hurriedly assured me that Mira was only in her second month of pregnancy at the time of her death.

Only Johnny was shrewd enough to guess that the tears were for myself. Knowing eyes held me across the room. Should I run or stay? With Johnny, there was too much excess baggage.

A New Start

As I looked out of the penthouse suite at Seven Seas, it reminded me of what life was like when Mira was around – an extended luxurious, sinful holiday, paid for by Uncle Kermani. But now I had to earn my keep.

It had been subtly conveyed to me that there would be no more generous monthly deposits to my personal account. An employee account had been opened in my name and a salary would be credited on the first of every month.

Mira had all the airs of an heiress, yet she chose to carve a name for herself in the world of finance, and something similar was expected of me. Her death had left a big void in Uncle Kermani's life. How the hell was I supposed to fill it? I am neither beautiful nor brilliant, fuck, I am not even sane most days. Most of my life had been spent holding a brush and clay to mould into shapely curves. How was I going to sit in a glass cabin, wearing a tie, and run a super luxury resort that had little use for me? How?

It was a classic Catch-22 situation: going back to London meant facing assault charges and staying in Monele meant a life of extreme comfort and unimaginable boredom.

Azaan, my boy, Uncle Kermani had you by the balls.

First day at work and I had done nothing but brood. Keeping up with the pretence was going to be rather difficult. A phone call from the great man's PA reminded me that a meeting was under way and I was supposed to have been there ten minutes ago.

I quickly donned a tie and made my way to the conference room. Old and middle-aged men were seated around the oval table going over figures. I took the chair next to the only young face in the room. Her name tag read 'Anna'; she seemed familiar but conversation was impossible at this moment.

The meeting broke up half an later, but not before Uncle Kermani formally introduced me as the new executive director, operations.

Congratulations poured in from all sides and it was decided that a grand weekend party would be held in my honour. Back in my cabin, I was about to loosen the noose when my glance fell on a burly fellow in tasteless clothes and a bad haircut propped on the sofa, looking out at the panoramic view.

'Excuse me, can I help you?'

'My name's Officer Ray, I'm investigating the murder of General Baines.'

'Ah, my next-door neighbour found beheaded in the kitchen garden.'

'So you are aware of the circumstances in which the body was found?'

'It's the only thing all the patients and the orderlies would talk about after your people dug him out.'

'Did you guys share a good rapport?'

'It's a tad difficult to have a conversation through those brick walls but we got by.'

'How was he taking it?'

'No one likes being locked up. He was fucking depressed.'

'His death can hardly be attributed to depression. Where were you the night the general was murdered?'

'Stuck in my hole of a room, 203. They watched me night and day like I was some lab animal. They wouldn't let me out of sight. I wasn't even allowed a phone call.'

'Really? Then how did you put a call through to the general's house?'

'I called from Mira's cell. She came to see me two days before her death. Unfortunately, the general was out at the time, and I spoke to the missus, but you already know that.' His eyes squinted into slits.

'What about Mira?'

'What about Mira? She's dead. You want to ask questions, you go ask that son-of-a-bitch doctor and what he did to her. Now get out of my office, now.'

He didn't leave immediately but stood and stared at me as I tried to suppress my rage. 'It's okay to mourn the loss of people we love.'

'There's nothing to mourn. I hated that bitch.'

Skeletons in the Closet

I was practically living in Monele now. The police guesthouse I stayed in was a painful reminder that I needed to wrap up the case and head home. The days passed quickly, interviewing suspects, reviewing information, but the evenings got lonely.

I missed my wife; she had spent a better part of her life looking after the house and the children, while my job took me to remote towns and seedy guesthouses. Life had simply passed us by.

I was not much of a drinker, but a peg of the local rum helped me sleep better. I figured a long time ago that rich man or poor, they are both lonely in the confines of their mind. So I didn't really mind the travelling and the lonely evenings. Frankly, in view of the company I was keeping, it only seemed fair that I experienced the loneliness of the drunks and the crazies. The rum was strong and burnt my throat. As I sipped it, I watched moths fly to the light bulb and, one by one, burn and fall to the ground – just like the thoughts that plagued my mind. I tried to shut them out, drive them away. As soon as the old ones went, new ones took their place. I sat down to smoke a cigarette and maybe write a line or two.

There's a secret doorway,
Through which they float in every night,
Like the moths chasing the light,
Dying, falling to the ground,
Morbid,
Sepia,
They have no texture,
Though a certain brooding quality,
Brings them to life,
Thoughts, millions of them,
Passing, entangled,
Real, only in the confines of the mind,
They overwhelm the dark, insane,
These strange thoughts, night after night.

These thoughts brought me face to face with the star of my murder investigation, Johnny Will: a hard man to pin down. Things seemed to have worked in his favour. The mounting evidence suggested he could not have killed Mira or the general. New players kept popping up.

The autopsy revealed that the general had alcohol and a small amount of morphine in his bloodstream, but the death was clearly due to decapitation. The drug had probably been used to make him drowsy and hence easy to dispose of. I now had two interlinked murders to solve, and a whole list of people to interview.

It was time to grill the nuts and bolts that kept the machinery of Thy Will running. I believed that information flowed from the bottom to the top.

The head orderly at the rehab, Sunny, is a tall fellow, built like a truck. He was a loud man, his answers downright rude. A man who knew he had a job to do and nothing to fear. I quickly led him through some of the routine questions and asked the more pertinent ones later.

'Are the inpatients allowed an out-pass to visit their family?'

'Not until Dr Will says so.'

'Maybe if they bribe one of the orderlies? There isn't much in the name of security here.'

'We locals are honest people, not like the filth that comes and stays here,' he said vehemently, too vehemently. So bribing an orderly could not be ruled out.

'Did Miss Kermani visit her cousin very often?'

'Once in a while. She was the only one who was allowed to visit patient 203 in his room. Otherwise, all visitors were to be seated in the foyer.'

'When was the last time she visited him?'

'The week she died.'

'Did she seem upset on her last visit?'

'No, sir, but she definitely had some good news to share because I heard 203 congratulate her.'

Could it be that Mira had confessed to Azaan about her lovechild?

'Did he seem happy after she left?'

'I can't really say, happy or sad, 203 was always kicking the walls, hurting himself or anyone who went in to calm him down. He alone has broken more fingers and jaws of the orderlies at Thy Will than any other patient in the last four years. Doctor Will says he's very dangerous.'

In Marie, I met another loyalist of the Will clan. A matronly figure, who refused to exercise her vocabulary beyond a terse yes or no, at least with me.

It was time for some shock therapy.

I took out the butcher's knife from my leather satchel and waved it in front of her. Her hand closed over her mouth in horror to suppress a scream; a predictable reaction at the sight of the dried blood casing a butcher's knife.

'Does this belong to your kitchen, ma'am?'

'Yes, it does. I have had it in my kitchen for twenty years.'

'Didn't you notice it missing?'

'No, it's kept in the bottom drawer of the third shelf by the sink. I don't really use it often.'

I pulled the drawer open. It was cluttered with all kinds of junk. I figured that unless someone knew where the knife was, it would be almost impossible to find it.

'How many people know where you keep the knife?'

'Besides me, Johnny, Zac and the she-devil, Adele. The knife has always been kept there since the days of Miss Daisy.'

'A woman couldn't have used the knife; drunk or not, the general was trained in unarmed combat.'

'I wouldn't be surprised if the old python put her son up to it.'

'You mean Zac? But why?'

She suddenly went quiet, having spoken too much.

'Marie, I can question you at the town police station, if you like. You could be there for a while for withholding imperative information in a police investigation.'

She cringed visibly. I didn't derive any pleasure from threatening old women, but I needed to get all the information

I could from her. When she spoke again, it was with the confidence of a woman who knew what she was talking about.

'According to the will, if Johnny disgraces himself or dies, Thy Will would pass to Zac.'

That was a strong motive.

'But why make such an elaborate plan when it would be simpler to kill Johnny?'

'The mother–son duo tried that many years ago. You see the scar on his chin, they tried to kill my boy and . . .' She struggled to get the words out. 'God will never forgive her, my child crippled for life.'

'Crippled?'

'Adele could not hide her joy when she returned from the hospital. The doctor told her that Johnny could never have children.'

This changed everything.

The case was getting murkier. Back in my room, I played the recorded interview of Adele Will. Her voice boomed in the room.

'No woman wants a half-a-man in her life or in her bed, not for long.'

I rummaged through my old records and found the report about Johnny being attacked by an unknown assailant, six months after his father's death.

There was too much confusion, too many suspects, each with a strong motive. There were too many old, unresolved issues, all somehow linked to Mira's murder. The Will family's sins of the past seemed to be rubbing on to the present.

I needed a new approach to the case. Flipping through the pages of my little diary, I jotted down the questions that bothered me the most.

Could Azaan's love–hate relationship with Mira have turned violent? He did seem like someone who had no control over his anger.

According to Marie, Adele and Zac had tried to kill Johnny once, could this be their second attempt to reclaim Thy Will, by framing Johnny for his fiancée's murder?

On the other hand, an unfaithful woman is enough to push a smart man like Johnny over the edge. Especially when the man has childhood traumas like an alcoholic father, a dead mother and a household bereft of love and affection.

Johnny's inability to sire children was merely the cherry on top.

The Inquisition

The dreaded day was here. Officer Ray and I shared a cup of coffee in the recreation room. The afternoon sun streamed through the windows. I kept picking at the jute threads coming out of the worn-out sofa while he went through his little notebook.

I had childish thoughts of grabbing the diary and making a run for it. In my mind, I saw him make an undignified leap to nab me, snatch his precious notebook and slap handcuffs around my wrists.

'Life couldn't have been easy for you after your doctor-husband was institutionalized?'

The question caught me off-guard. 'I didn't have a roof over my head, no money in the bank and no parents to run home to. Saying it wasn't "easy" would be an understatement,' I declared with some vehemence.

'I have heard neurologists earn great money. Yet, you say there was no money.'

'There was always plenty to spend, for wining and dining, buying the best of clothes, jewellery, but never anything in my name. I am not complaining; it was a good life.'

'What went wrong?'

'He got addicted and went bananas.'

'So you left him?'

'I couldn't do much, he had a stroke. I stuck around till I could and then his children and his ex-wife came and threw me out.'

'You mean wife?'

'What's the point in asking these questions if you already know the answers, Officer?'

'He never did marry you, right?'

'Wrong, he did; just forgot to mention that he hadn't bothered to divorce his wife. Apparently it was less expensive to remain married than get a divorce.'

'It must have been upsetting, to be a kept woman for so long and not know it.'

I cursed him inside my head. He had a knack for asking the nastiest questions. But I said nothing.

'So, you came to work for Johnny, away from the fancy life of a big city.'

'I like it here. It's a peaceful and straightforward life, at least it has been so far, away from the cheats and frauds of the world.'

'What about Mira? Were you friends? From what I hear, she used to visit the centre often.'

'We weren't even on first-name basis.'

'Why is that, Sera? Didn't you like her?'

'No. And you can write that in your little book!'

I was so angry I could barely speak. I thought of walking out, but he pre-empted me.

'I am going to give you five minutes to compose yourself and we'll give it another shot, Miss.'

Through the grills on the window, I saw him light a

cigarette right under the sign that read 'No smoking, no littering'.

While he puffed away, I tried a few breathing techniques in a vain attempt to calm myself. If I wasn't so angry, I would probably find the whole situation funny; to be a suspect in a murder investigation isn't an everyday happening. Five minutes on the watch, he was by my side.

'Tell me, how are things between Zac and Johnny?'

'Good.'

'Did Zac like Mira?'

'Oh yes,' I said, remembering how Zac had gone on and on about finding a replacement who was as good as Mira, professionally, the other night.

'Did Johnny mind Zac's association with Mira?'

'No, why would he?'

I looked at him. There was something that he knew about Zac and Mira that apparently I didn't.

'The baby's DNA is a forty per cent match.'

After my initial shock at hearing about Mira's pregnancy, I was reconciled to the fact that Johnny and she had made a baby.

'I am well aware of that.'

'The DNA test is pretty accurate, right?' he asked, and I nodded.

The only available technique used for conducting the DNA test in the 1990s was RFPL or rif-lip as it was popularly called. A test with a high accuracy rate, and forty per cent is high by any standards, as the foetus has fifty per cent of each partner's DNA.

'You think Zac could be the father?'

'That's the most ridiculous thing I have heard since you started speaking!'

'You don't know, do you, our genius doctor is sterile?'

Officer Ray shoved an old medical report in front of me. It clearly stated that Johnny had suffered from 'Blunt Testicular Trauma' and infertility was indeed a long-term side effect of it.

In great detail, the report described the injury caused and the action taken to repair it. It came as a shock, but that still didn't make Zac the father. It was impossible.

'Their mothers were sisters and Zac's DNA would be the closest to Johnny's, so you quickly jumped to the conclusion that the baby was Zac's?'

'Something on those lines, yes.'

'Let me tell you something, Officer, cousins really don't share that much DNA. Theoretically, first cousins inherit an average 12.5 per cent of DNA identical to ours. It is just an average. No two people, not even siblings, have the exact same DNA. Their DNA will be somewhat similar, but it will be different.'

'But wouldn't the percentage shoot up if the first cousin has the same father, Miss – strictly theoretical at this point, of course?'

I stared at him, dumbfounded. He had done his research. He was right about half-brothers sharing half of their DNA that came from the fathers' side. But no one knew who Zac's father was, or did they?

Why was Officer Ray so keen on discussing this information with me? Where was the tight-lipped policeman act?

Much as I tried, Officer Ray's attempts at friendliness only discomfited me further. He certainly didn't need my opinion as a doctor; he knew plenty already.

Confessions of a Deranged Mind

All that coughing made my throat dry and I absolutely hated the sight of red mucus on my pristine white handkerchief. Disgusting!

I put the kerchief in my pocket. In the narrow confines of the confessional and its mottled light, I knelt before God.

The mind has this tendency to wander in every direction except where one wants it to go. The coughs racked my body again and I longed for my herb tea. It had kept me going for so long.

My well-maintained body could be attributed to natural remedies and to wonderful genes. Of late, these genes were also responsible for the bone cancer that was slowly metastasizing throughout my body.

My mother had it; Daisy, of course, was fortunate enough to have escaped the disease by dying young.

My elation at her death had been short-lived. Robin was too far gone by then to have realized that we were now free to marry each other. It seemed like an ideal situation, where the younger sister had almost the licence to marry the widowed brother-in-law to raise her sister's son.

I had first laid eyes on him when I returned after completing my graduation. To a twenty-year-old, the attention of a man of the world seemed like stuff out of a romantic novel. Despite his infidelity, he continued living with Daisy, fathering a child and playing the dutiful, if not loving, husband.

On many nights, not long before his seed was in my belly, I had stayed awake and wondered if Robin loved me. I felt cheated. I had given up a respectable life to bear his child, waiting for him like an extra in the wings for the final curtain call that never came.

Our children were growing fast. While Zac was a good-natured boy, Johnny seemed to be cut from a different cloth altogether.

His perpetual frown and piercing eyes made me uncomfortable even when he was too young to cause any trouble. All that changed the day he saw Robin and me together. Daisy never spoke to me ever again.

My demand for his attention and Daisy's growing depression finally drove Robin to the bottle. I was a penniless, young mother, not altogether deserted by her lover, living in disgrace, at the charity of her sister. Going away was not an option, for in my heart I foolishly believed that Robin would someday muster up the courage to sever his marriage vows.

No one thought that I was as much the victim in this sordid affair, as was Daisy. Her marriage gave her the status of a martyr, while I became the temptress who had led him astray. My dreams didn't matter; I had stolen my sister's husband. I was to be punished for loving what wasn't rightfully mine.

Yet, I look back to the time it all began, when I was like

any other girl, guileless and seeking love. There flowed in my heart a feeling so sure, so pure that I was willing to embrace a life of shame to be with the man I loved. Fate, that mischief-maker, drew us together and then kept us apart, even though we lived under the same roof.

I was naïve then. It was hard to see Daisy wilting like a flower, yet what could I have done? You couldn't make people love you.

Even my own son is quick to judge, label. It never occurred to anybody that we were just two people who were pulled towards each other by something beyond our control.

Robin longed not just for my body, or the face they say is beautiful, he longed to be with me. To walk like two ordinary people up a hill hand-in-hand, or merely laugh together, to do a thousand things that couples did. Robin's death marked the end of a hope that had flickered dangerously for years. I was left with nothing but bitterness, the sum total of my life's possessions.

From Robin, from being with Robin, I learnt my greatest lesson; I learnt what love is not. Love isn't lust that coils below the stomach, it isn't 'me first', it isn't forced. Love is never scared, love is not pretence, never pretence. It's pure like the tears that still roll down my eyes when I think of him. It's chaste like the prayer that I sometimes offer God.

Love isn't shame. Love isn't moving on, it's being honest with ourselves. Was Robin honest with himself or Daisy? I remember what it was like after he returned to his sham of a marriage. He was like a circus monkey rattling the cage. Though I had let him go, I wondered at night if he buried his head in her lap, as he did in mine, faking an apology, expressing his love earnestly, just so he could shore things up, restore the normalcy of his marriage. Daisy was the ideal wife, loving, forgiving, hungry for the morsels of affection her husband threw at her.

With his old cheeriness, Robin jumped back into the role of a husband. But his eyes strayed like before. It was the first time I felt something akin to pity and disgust for the father of my child.

The old resentment had fermented over the years into the cancerous growth that would be my end. Telling Zac about my illness would be a comfort, but I did not want to risk seeing pain or pity in my son's beautiful eyes.

Despite a childhood spent hearing me rant and rave, Zac has turned out to be a fine, handsome fellow. The only thing I have managed to get right.

Still, there is much to do before I breathe my last. Half of the property rightfully belongs to Zac and he is going to have it, soon enough, I would see to that. Johnny could fool Zac with his ways, but not me. Everyone simply assumed that Johnny, the son of a wronged mother, would be the epitome of righteousness, and Zac, the fruit of the evil tree.

They couldn't be more wrong. A disturbed mind like Johnny's was programmed to mistrust and use people to further his own agenda.

My stupid son didn't realize that the only reason Johnny had not given his name to the police years ago was because I had threatened to drag Daisy's name through the mud. As a sixteen-year-old, Johnny had hated the thought of his mother's sorry life being exposed to public scrutiny and pity. Even in those days, he had fanciful ideas about himself and who he was going to become.

'Johnny, you rat on Zac and every man, woman and child

in this town will know how your poor mother couldn't keep your father by her side. Oh, but how she tried.' I had laughed in his face.

Johnny told the police nothing. But by keeping quiet, he manipulated Zac into believing that he cared for him more deeply than he had ever shown. I wasn't going to let him get away with my son's share of the fortune. He was going to pay up or go to jail.

There, I confessed it all!

The Quarry

The jade cufflinks went well with the off-white shirt and steel-grey trousers, a gift from Mira on some frivolous occasion. She loved to give gifts and was always buying something for someone.

I smiled at the memory of her enthusiasm when she handed over the gift-wrapped cufflinks to me. Now, the cufflinks reminded me of life's fullness when she had been around.

Pushing the thought away, I picked up the invite and walked towards my study. The exquisite envelope bore the famous Seven Seas insignia of an angel inviting one to follow.

I had received very many invitations from them in the past and had hardly ever bothered to attend, but today was different. I wanted to observe Azaan's behaviour. The party was to begin at eight and it was a quarter past seven. My date was ready and waiting in the study.

Today, I could smell her perfume from a mile away. I knew the fragrance, I had gifted it to her last Christmas. A knee-length, white dress with a crimson stole across one shoulder – Sera's virginal white was tempting.

'Shall we?' I offered her my arm.

'Are we running late?' she asked, taking it reluctantly.

'Not if I drive like a maniac.'

'I would like my hair to stay in place,' she said, smoothing an imaginary strand and smiling.

'Well, there are more ways than one to spoil your hairdo,' I challenged.

'That can wait.'

'And what if I am not willing to wait?'

'Then I'll just have to fix it again.'

Our relationship had changed, gone was the reluctant Sera of yesterday; in her place stood a woman willing to risk her heart. Her high expectations from finer emotions like love were misplaced, but it was a lesson I did not wish to teach her. During the quiet drive through the hilly roads, I concluded that life's a seductress in a slinky dress bumping into you just when you decided it was time you got your act straight.

I wanted once again the magic of holding hands, walking down a secluded beach, staring into the night sky, whispering sweet nothings. I wanted, above all, to lose myself in her straight black hair and trusting eyes. Yet, getting involved with Sera romantically could only have disastrous consequences for her.

My name was not yet cleared in the murder investigations and there had been a long silence from Ray's end. That, to me, was a sign that all was not well.

Hadn't he come around to question the staff at Thy Will the other day? What information could he have gleaned from Marie and the orderlies? Nothing that would put a nail in my coffin, as far as I could tell. Surely, Sera would have said something if that were the case.

'Since when did you start paying house calls to your patients, Johnny?' Sera brought me back to the present.

'I want to see how my patient behaves in an uncontrolled environment exposed to multiple stimuli.'

'Stop treating Azaan as a test subject of some twisted experiment.'

'I am just testing a theory I have.'

'Amuse me.'

'Uh, he's going to make a play for you.'

'Excuse me?'

'He'll try and win you over so that he can manipulate you to get to me.'

'Well, you may find it hard to believe, Johnny, but men do find me attractive,' Sera said angrily.

Since they were children, Azaan and Mira had been repeatedly told that they were betrothed to each other. While Mira grew out of it in time, Azaan continued to view her as his precious possession. Kermani, a shrewd businessman, gauged the situation and sent Azaan packing to London to pursue a course in Fine Arts. Kermani thought separating the two would bring them closer, that Mira would eventually begin to miss him.

They flourished in their respective fields: Mira as a financial consultant and Azaan as an upcoming artist. Kermani believed that the great union was now just a matter of time. And then began Azaan's bouts of explosive behaviour. Six months after I started dating Mira, Kermani brought Azaan to my facility for the first time.

It didn't take Azaan long to figure out that Mira and I were seeing each other. The doctor–patient rapport was never sufficiently established because he viewed me as a rival for Mira's affection.

The treatment was doomed from the beginning, yet saying no to Kermani was not an option, especially when Azaan was a wanted man in the UK. Admission in a mental facility kept him safe from the clutches of law.

Sera didn't need to know all this; she was after all the bait with which I planned to reel in Azaan. Azaan, Mira's mystery lover.

There was a huge gathering in the lawn by the lake created by a famous landscape artist. Vases filled with chrysanthemums were placed all around, glittering lights hung from trees, pruned to resemble animal heads – an elephant, a giraffe, a kangaroo and a bear.

Waiters curtsied to the guests in their impeccable white uniforms. A slight breeze added to the gaiety of the evening. A piece of instrumental music played softly, as wine, whisky and canapés moved about on silver platters. One could hardly miss the somewhat disproportionate sculptures of female forms sculpted by the great Azaan. People huddled together to discuss his art; one sculpture had a woman's toe touching her boob, not quite the Nataraja pose. It was grotesque!

Sera was certainly taken in by the surroundings and exclaimed loudly when she saw a sculpted mermaid, with a tiny waist and breasts like melons, languishing by the lake. 'He's talented!'

Enamoured by the sculpture, she hurried to get a closer look, leaving me behind to sample the fine white offering from Kermani's famous wine cellar.

I saw Anna coming towards me with outstretched arms. I

had not seen her since Mira's death. She looked hot in a fitting dress, but sadly nothing could be done about her mature, over-painted face.

'Hi, Johnny, it's been a while.'

'Hey, Anna, you look lovely.'

'Thanks, how have you been? I mean, with the police investigation and the rumours . . .'

'Haven't heard any.'

'I understand. It wouldn't help to hear that you murdered your pregnant girlfriend.'

I could barely control my anger but managed to fake a smile. 'Who needs enemies when they have well-wishers like you.'

'Johnny, I am sorry it came out like that. If there's anything I can do . . .'

'Sure, just watch your mouth around me,' I said, drifting away from her, but she didn't let me.

'Say hello to Zac for me, I hear you keep him busy running errands for you.'

Bitch, she sounded so much like Aunt Adele.

'That's what he gets paid for, Anna.'

'Yes, but it must be such a comfort to know that there is someone you can rely on to look after your affairs . . .' Her voice trailed off.

That sounded ominous. Could Anna be contemplating becoming Mrs Zac Will? That would explain her spurious concern for my well-being. Zac, my brother, you could do without another Adele in your life.

'You are here with your assistant?' she asked. Getting away from her wasn't going to be easy.

'Sera is not my assistant, she's a qualified . . .'

'Oh, it's funny how one remembers things. Mira once said to me, "I seriously don't understand why Johnny doesn't just hire a proper secretary."' A false laugh accompanied the reverie.

'Thanks for sharing Mira's memorable words, I feel so much better talking to you, Anna.' The sarcasm was totally lost on her. Anyway, with that, I wriggled out of her company in search of Sera.

She stood exactly where I had left her, deep in conversation with our host.

'This is pure genius!'

The awe in Sera's voice nearly made me choke on the wine. Genius and madness run together, I wanted to tell her.

In those expensive collared black shirt and well-cut trousers, Azaan looked a lot older than he was. He exuded an air of confidence that would have most women swooning and our Sera was no exception. The effect of what Azaan was saying to Sera in hushed tones was not lost on me.

'Kind of you to accept my invitation,' I heard Azaan say to my date.

'I'm here with Johnny. Congratulations, this is a great start, becoming a director, having your own office . . .'

'I hate glass cabins, closed spaces suffocate me.'

'It may all seem a little overwhelming at first, but soon you'll adjust into your new routine,' Sera said in her usual soothing tone.

'I am not one of your retards at the rehab, don't use that condescending tone with me.' Azaan flared up – a perfect example of IED in motion, harmless statement, strong reaction.

The thought of intervening crossed my mind, but Sera could look after herself.

'Then maybe you should spend the evening with your enchanting statues that can't talk back.'

'Ever been locked up, Doc? Eaten tasteless food and been strapped to your bed? I don't think so.'

Sera's reply was very matter-of-fact. 'No, but I have cared for enough of them.'

'So you care for me?'

'I do, as doctors, we . . .'

'Shut the fuck up, you doctors love playing God to the sick and the lonely.'

An angry Sera turned to go. She would have walked away all high and mighty had it not been for Azaan's hand that caught her wrist. She tried to pull her hand back, but his grip was firm and the look in his eyes positively demonic.

Sera cursed under her breath and pulled with all her might. Just at that moment, Azaan decided to let go. She lost her balance and, before the great sculptor could catch her, fell.

He bent down to pick up the furious Sera. Her white dress had mud stains and she looked ready to burst into tears. I marched down the slope to rescue her.

'You didn't hurt yourself, did you?'

'No, Johnny, remember it's clumsy Sera!' she said through clenched teeth.

Azaan and I looked on as she struggled to get the mud off her dress. I had this sudden urge to pick her up and take her home, but not before I had given the rude fucker a piece of my mind.

'How is it that women are always stumbling around you, Azaan?'

'At least, they don't end up dead, Doc.'

Anna had eaten up my reserve of composure for the day and Azaan was the last straw. I punched him in the face and he staggered backwards, blood trickling from his nose. He retaliated with a right hook that knocked the wind out of me. Our little skirmish must have caught some attention, for the next instant Kermani appeared and said, formally, 'Gentlemen.'

At that moment, I wanted to kill Azaan, or at least cause enough injury to wipe that smug smile off his face.

'Mira would have not been too proud of your little outburst, Doc.'

I grabbed Azaan by the collar and said, 'Would you like to join her?'

Kermani, probably horrified at the thought of losing his heir, asked me firmly to leave the premises.

'I warned you, Kermani, he's a sick man in need of treatment.'

'Johnny, you don't appear too lucid either right now. You should leave.'

He was right. My top shirt button was undone, the longish hair must have appeared unkempt and I had just violated the doctor–patient agreement by threatening a patient, that too, in front of a sizeable audience.

Sera, having never seen me lose control like that, was quiet on our way back.

'Johnny, was it necessary?'

'No, but life's a bitch; it happens. Get used to it, Sera,' I snapped at her.

My hands were behind the wheel, but my mind stumbled through my memories, charting a journey that began with the death of the patriarch of the Will household. It all began at seven every evening, the soda, the icebox, an expensive crystal tumbler.

He sat by his favourite place in the study, listening to some regional music on the radio. He cared two hoots about the music, but it seemed to lend a semblance of credibility to his claim of 'enjoying the routine evening drink'.

The cuckoo clock struck every hour and Robin could be heard bellowing all the way past the empty servant quarters. He cursed my mother for keeping him trapped in a loveless marriage. Some evenings when he was being particularly spiteful, he did a perfect mimicry of my mother: 'I love you to death, Robin, and I don't care if you don't love me back. I am not going to divorce you; not in this life!'

At times, he bad-mouthed Adele for ruining his life, for passing someone else's trash as his. 'I know what are you like. You wanted it, you got it, now get out of my life.'

I wasn't spared either. I'd get blamed for being an ungrateful child, a fucking liability like my mother. He harped on similar themes every single evening, at times vindictive, at others playing the victim – how he had sacrificed so much to keep his family together, yet here he was sitting and drinking alone, disgraced and cut off from the world.

He somehow had a seemingly rational explanation for every evil that had befallen us, including why his wife had to die when help was at hand.

My mother had given up on life, she didn't wish to live anymore and when the opportunity presented itself, she embraced it with the calm of a saint. Sometimes, I think he was a decent man torn between his love for Adele and his sense of duty towards Mother and me. Would things have worked out better if he had walked out on us rather than endure a loveless marriage?

What makes a man marry one woman and love another?

What makes a woman lie in the arms of one man and dream of another?

The big question is, what is the right choice? The one where you put out the tormenting fire of your desire to keep your vows, or relinquish old claims to make new ones? Build the sound foundation of a brand-new home on the grave of old relationships and carry around the guilt of hurting another for the rest of your life?

Here I am, ready to seduce Sera to fill the void Mira has left, but what of Sera's feelings that run far deeper than mine? It isn't an equal exchange; one of us is going to be hurt and it won't be me, not again, not ever.

I walked Sera to the outhouse; she waited for me to say something.

'Sera . . .'

'What?'

'Never mind.' I turned to go.

'Say it, Johnny.' Her eyes were clouded with want.

'Lock the door at night.'

Sera mistook the concern in my voice to be passion and said, 'Locks are easy to pick if someone is willing to risk their neck.'

I stroked her slender neck and said, 'I believe someone is willing.'

I cupped her breast, and through the soft fabric of her dress, her puckered nipples showed. She stood still, waiting for me to invite her in. I didn't, I couldn't; she would hate me in the morning. I couldn't make love to her in my present state of mind. I just wanted to fuck. We stared at each other a long time before I left her standing, aware of the sound of my own laboured breathing.

The Suspect List

'You must have been madly in love to marry a man fifteen years your senior.'

'Just plain broke. Marriage at that time meant security, and besides, he was a very charming man.'

'So you married him for his charm and when it ran out, you left.'

'His charm ran out much before the stroke. That was just the last straw. His awful, greedy children have made the best health care available for him. They didn't need an expensive nurse like me.'

'But the stroke came much later. Wasn't he admitted for a morphine overdose before that?'

'Yes, but if you would care to dig some more, he had also overdosed on barbiturates the year before that and almost died.'

'Had he died of the overdose, it would have worked out very well for you.'

'We have been there before, haven't we, Officer? I did not administer the morphine to him, if that is your roundabout way of asking.'

'I am merely pointing out that a rich widow is far more attractive to men than a penniless divorcee.'

'I am tired of your accusations. I wasn't legally married to him. The money wouldn't have come to me anyway.'

'But you didn't know it then, did you?'

Sera's face said it all. A flash of anger passed like lightning and disappeared as fast.

'Alright, that's pretty much it. I was actually calling upon Johnny when I saw the flowers at your doorstep.'

'What flowers?'

I walked over to the dining table and lifted a bouquet of the loveliest blue roses that I had ever seen. That Sera was perplexed is an understatement; she rushed to examine the flowers. A smile crossed her face, but her mind rejected the identity of the sender.

'You see, the flowers gave me the idea maybe you have a new admirer.'

'About time.' She gave me an enigmatic smile and climbed the stairs leading to her room.

Fine, so she wasn't going to tell me who had sent those flowers. I knew where to go. There was only one florist on the main avenue who could put together such a fine arrangement. I knew this because the orchids found in Mira's apartment had come from the same florist and he had claimed to receive the order on the phone from a man with a heavy accent.

Azaan Kermani had an accent.

I made my way back to the main house in search of Johnny. Three weeks since he walked out a free man. In three weeks, I had made much progress. Though I was still not sure if Johnny was involved or innocent, the skeletons were tumbling out fast from the closet. I now believed that Mira's death was premeditated, but the general's death was not part of the plan.

The stab wounds were not the work of a very sharp mind, but of an unstable one.

At first glance, it appeared the body had been very carefully hidden under the pile of manure.

While it didn't take a genius to figure out that manure would mask the foul smell of decay, it did require certain cunning to have buried the body where it could have been easily discovered.

The infamous Adam's Edge lay behind Thy Will. The body could have been easily rolled down the slope and wild animals would have devoured the body in no time, leaving no trace of the general or the stab wounds.

Maybe Johnny was right. There was someone out to get him. It was getting complicated; my suspect list was growing by the day, Johnny being the forerunner, followed by Zac, Azaan and Sera.

There was nothing even remotely ordinary about these people; they all had traumatic pasts and it was not easy to gauge what went on in their devious minds. Sera appeared to be serene and mature, but I had witnessed a streak of jealousy and obsession in her. Well, only time would tell how far off the mark I was in reading these people.

Walking through the narrow path up to the main house, I saw Johnny squatting in the kitchen garden, plucking tomatoes and placing them in a basket. It was warm enough for sweat to trickle down all the unlikely places and I wondered why he was out in the sun.

'They aren't ripe or juicy enough to be plucked yet.'

'A tomato needn't be ripe to be rotten from the inside, just like a man doesn't have to be guilty to be hounded by the police.'

I ignored the last bit and asked him about the tomatoes. I was curious. 'How do you know which ones to pluck? They all look the same.'

He picked up a green, shiny tomato and sliced it open and there it was, an insect tunnel running through the centre, colouring seeds black and dry.

'My childhood was spent in the kitchen garden, planting carrots, digging potatoes out. The garden was my mother's life and I have inherited her passion.'

'She wouldn't have been too pleased to find drunks and crazies ploughing her garden to de-stress.'

'Skip the niceties, Officer. What do you want to know?'

'Could Sera have injected Mira with morphine?'

'No, she's sane and *you* are crazy.'

'How about Frankenstein? Could Azaan have killed Mira?'

'Frankenstein, huh?' Johnny grinned and for a moment we shared a laugh, but then Johnny went back to plucking tomatoes.

'Yes, it's highly likely, but there is just one problem, he was locked up right under my nose.'

'How about Adele Will? Could she have harmed Mira?'

'For all her acid tongue, Adele is harmless. The old python has a lot of venom in her, but she's too lazy to go hunting herself.'

Marie had addressed Adele in a similar fashion; the

bonding between the cook and the master of the house was strong indeed.

'Could Zac be the father of Mira's child?'

'Bullshit!'

'But his DNA would be a match considering the close family connection . . . and your medical history.'

'I don't trust the tests you do in those shabby police labs. For a hundred bucks, you could be the father of Mira's child, Officer Ray.'

'You doubt the test, but trust your brother, eh?'

'Frankly, Zac doesn't have the balls to do it.'

'Screw her or kill her?'

'Either.'

'You forget he did bust your balls a few years ago.'

Johnny's face turned ashen. Abruptly his hand came up and he shook mine rather forcefully. 'I'm going to miss you.'

Confused, I asked, 'Where are you going?'

'Hawaii, for two weeks, to attend a medical conference.'

'You can't leave the country, Johnny! You are a suspect in a murder investigation. Actually two!'

'Thanks for reminding me but my bail has been posted by Kermani, and it says short of murdering people or robbing banks, I can do as I please.'

With that he turned and took the narrow path back home, leaving me to stare at the rotten tomato he had placed in my palm.

SERA

Pheromones at Work

The hills never went anywhere; they stood exactly where you had left them. There is something reassuring about their presence. After dark, the hill people don't like to venture out. The chances of accident on the narrow roads are high, and by five the shops shut and supper preparations begin. One never feels lonely among the hill people; they are hardworking and self-contained, and the evenings mean it's time to put up your feet and soak in the warmth from the fireplace.

In four years, I had never ventured this far out, but today I was restless, disturbed. What lay at the bottom of the steep valley? From this height, the valley seemed dressed in green, lost in hush.

The silence was beautiful, broken at times by the wings of a playful bird wanting to dive. A homeless mist would seek shelter, but would be kicked out by the last light before it could settle down.

Adam's Edge looked inviting. Not one to scare easily, I edged closer to the point from where, if I were to lose my footing, there would be precious little left to sew together and put in a casket, let alone a funeral.

But a woman with her head full of desire doesn't die that easy.

The phone call had come late in the evening and Marie had rushed to inform me that the phone in the study had rung for me. Thinking it to be Zac, I chirped a bright hello only to hear Johnny's voice on the line.

The conversation was stilted; about the patients, their medication. I pressed my ear closer to the receiver, in case I missed an inflection in his voice that would tell me of his deeper feelings for me. Nada.

Disappointed, I was about to hang up when he said, 'Can I bring you something from here?'

'Just come back soon,' I blurted out with great feeling and instantly regretted as he responded, 'Miss me, huh?'

'Am I allowed to?'

And he began to sing, '*Miss me every summer night and I shall make sweet love to you, dearest, when I return. Burn in my absence, dress for me, play with my name, call me home.*'

I had stayed like that for a long time after he had gone. The buzz of the receiver became the hum of the song.

I just couldn't let go of the promise in those verses; unbidden, the song played on my lips as I stood at Adam's Edge lost in a dream, and so didn't know when he came up behind me. Like bands of steel, the arms held me tight from behind. I had never known such fear before. I tried to scream but the words wouldn't come out. Warm breath fanned my nape; the ragged breathing was the only sound as I felt him inhale my scent. It was him, yes, it had to be him. A woman knows a man's touch.

'Please . . .' My voice sounded tearful even to my ears.

'Please what?'

Though the whisper was without menace, I could not stop myself from shuddering.

'Scared that I'll push you and no one will know, Sera?'

Blood rushed to my brain the minute I heard him utter my name. I drove my elbow fiercely into his ribcage.

Azaan screamed, but didn't let go of me.

'Rclease me this minute, you . . .' I tried to swallow my fear. You don't want to be threatening an IED patient at the edge of a valley.

'You land quite a punch, Doc.'

He released me but not before he had flicked the pin that held my hair together. The wind was mad enough to blow the hair on to my face, in my mouth, my eyes. I could not see.

Torn between wanting to fight Azaan and my hair, I picked the smaller battle.

'Hand me the pin.'

'Why, you look lovely like this.'

'The pin!' I glared at him.

He gave it back and watched me struggle to secure my hair. I turned to give him a piece of my mind. He simply stood there with a mischievous grin on his face.

'I am not one of your women friends to fool around with, Azaan!'

'Come out with me and I'll show you.'

'I don't go out with boys barely past puberty, with temper issues.'

'I am a full-blooded, able-bodied guy. And apart from some minor issues in life, I am your average guy. Mira would tell you that, Doc.'

Average guys don't go around breaking glass bottles in their girlfriend's face, I thought.

'Well, Mira wasn't your doctor and I am sure you never tried to push her down a steep valley.'

'What do you know, Doc?'

His reply made me step back. Officer Ray had asked me enough questions about Azaan and his routine at the rehab for me to gather he was a suspect in Mira's mysterious death. I longed to be back in the safe confines of Thy Will.

'I need to go. My patients must be waiting for me.'

I started to walk past him when his hand caught my wrist.

For a fraction of a second, I froze.

'How dare you do that, you spoilt brat?'

'Well, it's my uncle's money that's paying your salary, and besides that you have already wasted fifteen minutes of my therapy session.'

Then it struck me that it was the second Tuesday of the month and Azaan was here for his session. Not finding me in the office, he must have asked around and come looking for me.

Technically, I was in the wrong, but I wasn't going to admit it.

'There wasn't any need for these childish games; you could have sent one of the orderlies to get me.'

'I read somewhere that patients suffering from psychological disorders respond better to treatment in an open environment. I like it here, sweetheart.'

'I am nobody's sweetheart! Johnny isn't here and your uncle's money doesn't intimidate me. In future, you creep up on me like that and I'll have you locked up again.'

His face turned pink and I took a step backwards, thinking this time I had gone too far. I could see the capillaries popping on his forehead. Suddenly his eyes narrowed to slits, he sat down on the ground and started laughing.

I stared at him in confusion. What if I needed to shout for help? I looked around. And then it struck me. Help for what? My patient was laughing like a mad man. Not exactly reason enough to sedate him. I waited till the laughter subsided and asked him to follow me.

'I will, but I need your help. I don't feel so good.'

'Strange, you were just threatening me and now you can't even get up from the ground.'

'I feel faint, Doc.'

When I received no reply, I gave him my hand. His hand was cold and clammy. He wasn't lying! I let him lean on my shoulder and we started the steep walk home. He was heavy and I began to sweat despite the nip in the air. He must have noticed, for he straightened himself and mumbled, 'I'm fine now.' But he was far from fine and my doctor's instinct had resurfaced. I refused to let go of him.

'It's ironic how a few minutes back you were struggling in my arms and now you want me to cling to you.'

'I could dump you right now, Azaan, but the ethics of my profession forbid me to do that.'

'Quite an ethical lady you are. Mira had no ethics. Maybe that was why she and Johnny got along so well. What do you think?'

'I think you should conserve your energy till we get back. We still have a quite a distance to go.'

'I heard you've worked here for four years and haven't dated anyone. Why the celibate lifestyle? Don't you miss it?' He winked at me.

'Shut up! It's none of your business! You've been asking people about me?'

'I was just doing my homework. You were hardly going to divulge your boring little life's details to me, so I made some enquiries. I want you to pose for me.'

'I am twenty-nine and I like the way I live. I am not posing for anyone and, beyond a humane concern, I have no interest in you.'

He slid his hand around my waist, jerked me towards him, and the next thing I knew he was kissing me. Stunned by the impact of his lips on mine, I tried to turn my head, but he held it in place. He didn't seem so feeble now, and I cursed myself for my initial assessment of his frail state.

Then again, nothing adventurous had happened to me in the last four years. Tired of the tiny morsels Johnny threw my way, I decided to be reckless and for once threw caution to the wind. The fact that Azaan could kiss was the deciding factor. Most men watch too many movies and still don't get it right.

I kissed him back.

Our passionate drama would have gone on had fate not brought Adele Will to Adam's Edge that evening.

'We have company,' Azaan whispered in my ears.

Hastily I stepped away and looked in the direction from which a lone figure dressed in black was coming our way.

'Oh, damn, that's Adele Will, Johnny's Aunt,' I said in dismay.

'Well, the more the merrier.' He seemed not in the least disturbed.

Coming up to us she flashed her beautiful smile. 'Hello Sera, lovely evening, isn't it? I never knew you liked to come here.'

'Neither did she, apparently.' Azaan's voice held a subtle, sly note.

'Who might you be, young man?'

'Azaan.'

'Sera, you never mentioned you have a beau?'

'Oh no, Ms Will, it's not like that, he's a patient and we are getting late.'

Damn, why did I say that? I quickly walked away from her, hoping Azaan would follow suit, but he continued speaking to her. I was fuming by the time he caught up with me.

'What did you say to her?'

'Nothing. On the contrary, she said, "You must be quite a ladies' man to have our old maid Sera exchange a kiss in the wild."' He mimicked Adele Will to perfection.

'That old bitch! Now she'll go and spit it out to Johnny.'

'What's to worry about, Johnny is out of your league and you did kiss me back.'

In that moment, I wholeheartedly agreed with Johnny that Azaan could very well be a psychopath.

Lady Harding's Asylum

I was lost in the corridors of the grey-stone institution that dated back to the British era. My footsteps echoed around the high ceilings and sprawling rooms; doors stood open everywhere. The beds were lined up side by side, each separated from the other by faded cotton curtains. Salt-and-pepper heads resting on high beds, eyes vacantly staring at the dance of the dust particles in the sunlight.

Where was my man in this crowd?

A nursing attendant was giving an old man a shot in his wriggly, fat ass. Not a pretty sight, but I had a feeling that this was the daily morning routine and many more bums would be exposed. I waited for him to finish.

'Excuse me, I have come to see Dr Dhar. Which bed is he on?' I flashed my badge.

'There is no doctor here by that name.'

'Oh, no, I mean he's a patient and is also a doctor.'

'What's he got?'

'A stroke, I suppose.'

'Okay, you are looking for that cranky old man on bed number 40. Go straight and turn left. Last room around the door.'

'He can talk, right?'

'He talks alright.'

Then a patient shouted for the attendant and he left in a huff.

It was a private room, so he was its sole occupant. It seemed the children had been generous with the money and kept the old man in comfort. No such luck for Sera though. The old man was ageing gracefully despite the stroke. Now I could see why Sera had been attracted to him.

His hair was cut short and he was clean shaved. He was doing what generally patients do in the hospital, looking at the door. He saw me come in and his face lit up.

'Good morning, I am Officer Ray.'

'Many mornings are spent waiting, yet she never walks through that door.'

'Ah, so that's how you spend your time here, absorbed in poetry. I am a poet myself, a lesser known one though.' I smiled, he didn't.

'Tell me about Sera, your wife.'

'A cheap fruit trying to be a kiwi.'

'Does it bother you that she left you after you had a stroke?'

'Kiwis are Sera's favourite. She has expensive tastes, unlike the dowdy place she hails from.'

Something wasn't right. Still, I persisted. 'Did Sera have anything to do with your morphine overdose?'

'Give Sera a butcher's knife and she can slice the kiwi thin.'

I stored away that little piece of information, Sera and the butcher's knife. It was found near both murder victims.

'Could she have harmed you in any way?'

'The ruthless bitch cut my heart out like it were a kiwi fruit.'

I went in search of the nursing attendant.

'Does he have any lucid moments in the day? I could come back . . .' I stretched my hands to state my confusion.

The attendant laughed. 'No, there aren't any. He suffers from sensory aphasia. He speaks fluently, if you noticed?'

'Yes, I did.'

'Well, it's gibberish. He hears you alright but doesn't understand you. His brain functions have suffered severely. He says whatever comes to his mind.'

I cursed my luck. I'd driven all the way to the hospital for nothing. But gibberish or not, he wasn't a big fan of Sera's. He had called her a cheap fruit and a ruthless bitch. It wouldn't be admissible in a court of law, but it helped me draw my own conclusions.

The old doctor had married a penniless girl who had left him at the first sign of trouble. You add all that up and the story that emerges isn't pretty. She was just an opportunist. Could an opportunist get rid of another woman to secure her future? Yes, I think so.

The Old Stock

If someone had said there is some great conspiracy at work at Thy Will, I wouldn't have believed them – up until this morning that is. Much had changed in the past ten minutes.

The number and the words danced on paper as they must have to a dyslexic child. My mind was able to grasp the significance of what I was reading, but its ramifications were a different ball game.

To make that phone call or not was the big question now. Officer Ray would jump out of his chair at the information that I was about to give him.

I checked again. Three boxes of morphine had been ordered in April; one box contained ten ampoules of 20 mg each. Used primarily to relieve a patient suffering from acute pain, such as in accident cases, deep wounds etc., morphine wasn't really needed in a rehabilitation centre, especially as it was difficult to wean patients away from it because of its addictive qualities, the last thing a junkie needed.

Instead, methadone is used, which comes from the same family and is less addictive; Johnny mostly recommends that. Officer Ray had examined the hospital records and every ampoule had been accounted for. Our records were straight. The morphine in Mira or the general's body could not have come from the rehab.

But then again morphine is not an over-the-counter drug and that compounded Ray's problem. He may not know that we had ordered morphine so recently, but he may have assumed we have access to it. The way it would look to the officer, a big fat finger pointed in Johnny's direction.

My day had begun with taking inventory and checking the expiry of the drugs, which I did every three months. In doing so, I had accidentally picked up an ampoule of morphine whose expiry did not match the expiry of the remaining eight ampoules. Implying that the ampoule was part of the lot ordered last year.

On checking last year's records, I found two boxes had been carried forward, that took the count to five boxes, and not only the three we procured recently. Two boxes containing 400 mg of morphine were missing and unaccounted for. There was no record to show that either Johnny or Sera had requested for it.

Shit! We were in deep shit.

Worried, I picked up the phone and called Sunny and asked him to come down to my office. It wasn't as fancy as Johnny's, but that was by choice. Johnny was a bit of a show-off, while I liked to keep a low profile, something that didn't go down well with Adele, of course.

Sunny barged in a minute later. I wasn't really fond of this fellow – he had an air of arrogance which wasn't pleasing, but Johnny had left the running of the entire psyche ward to him. Who was I to question his capabilities then?

'Morning, Sunny, can you show me the record for any request for two boxes of morphine?'

'Two boxes of morphine? No one asked for them, sir.'

'As store in-charge, you issue the prescription medicines as requested, don't you?'

'Yes, sir, but neither Doctor Will nor Doctor Sera ordered any in the past two months, and I personally checked the three intact boxes.'

Exasperated, I said, 'But that's this year's quota, what about the remaining from last year? The total should be five and not three.'

I called Sera. She was just finishing breakfast and told me the same thing; no such emergency had arisen this past year that called for the use of morphine.

'Are you sure you didn't just go and pick up an ampoule and use it on a patient? Perhaps you don't remember.'

'I would remember, Zac; we are here to save people, not overdose them on morphine. You are forgetting I am a psychologist, I can't really prescribe medicines. I am your brother's pet; I do his bidding.'

She seemed upset that I should question her about the morphine, but not once did she ask why I was making such inquiries.

'Sera, any idea when Johnny is back?'

'I don't know.'

Sera's voice seemed to say – today, tomorrow, next week, she didn't care.

Adele had been at her bitchiest best at the dinner table recounting how Sera had been kissing one of her patients at Adam's Edge.

I didn't believe her at first because the description of the 'beau' sounded much like Azaan. And Sera had her eyes set on Johnny; it was definitely steamy in Johnny's study the other night. Still, I had seen Azaan around practically every day since Johnny left. He didn't seem the type who would be so enthusiastic about his treatment.

It could be that Azaan had taken a fancy to Sera, a woman who knew a thing or two about the human mind and anatomy. An irresistible combination for a loose cannon like Azaan. Anyway, what if Johnny had taken the boxes? If he had, he was hardly likely to confess. Killers and confessions were not words you often heard together. And if he hadn't?

This puzzle needed to be dumped in Ray's lap, but a little voice urged me to let sleeping dogs lie. Even a nitwit could tell the missing ampoules meant the killer was closer home than imagined. I decided to sleep over it. A delicious meal at Anna's place, a good night's sleep on her cushy mattress and a back rub was bound to give the whole thing a fresh perspective.

Adele watched me from the door as I exercised on the floor. A few hundred push-ups and two hundred crunches left me huffing.

She continued staring at my chest. 'Your father was a very fit man; he could do at least another hundred at your age.'

Adele rarely spoke to me about him. She was definitely getting old.

'It didn't help him much, did it? A man setting himself on fire isn't exactly my idea of a father figure.'

'You have so much anger against him, Zac, and you didn't know him like I did.'

'You did, Mother! Why don't you feel angry? That coward was screwing you in the same house, and didn't have the guts to stand up for you or me.' I exploded.

'No, he didn't. He was a nice man, but had no spine. Nevertheless, he loved me.' Her voice carried emotions from a faraway time.

'Not much good his love did to you. You are old, bitter and . . .'

'Dying.'

'What, what did you say?'

I couldn't stop myself from laughing, Adele has always had this thing for melodrama. 'Mother, you have been dead a long time. I don't remember the last time you laughed or cried for that matter. If that is love, I don't want any of it.'

'If you keep seeing that selfish chit Anna, I doubt you'll ever know what it means.' She ignored my outburst. 'Zac, learn to fix your closet, I might not be around for long to fix it for you.'

I looked around the room, not a thing out of place. She followed my gaze to the single elaborately carved unmade bed, to the pile of self-help books (which Adele totally derided; she would say, 'What do you need help for, Zac?') and finally to the glass of protein shake on the table. It was as tidy as it could be.

Mother was simply a control freak, something I had figured long ago.

The mumbling didn't reach her, but my expression must have, because she gave me one of her twisted smiles and left me to get ready for my date.

On my way to Anna's house, I couldn't help wondering what had gotten into Adele. I had never known her to be vulnerable, mother-like.

Or maybe it was just me, the bitter fruit of a bitter tree, doubting every word, every innocuous gesture, everyone.

Mr Lonely

Days had stretched into weeks. The stupid lawyers had me buried in paperwork. Having too much money can be a pain. I wished to give all of it away, except the house, of course.

The sight of mist settling over Thy Will made me marvel at how wonderfully different life was in this small town. The cab dropped me at the main entrance, but no one rushed out to meet me. No one knew I would be coming today.

Maybe this was why people kept dogs. I longed for a dog's loving welcome, lapping up remembered scents. How lonely it could get. No one to greet a man when he came home after two weeks; my life was beginning to get to me.

The aura around Thy Will seemed strange, quieter than usual, almost like death. No, I thought, no more unfortunate deaths were happening on my property. I thought of calling Officer Ray, but abandoned the idea as soon as it came. He was the enemy. I was confident he would have gathered enough ammo by now to shoot me at sight. I desperately needed some friends; family was out of question, or was it? Maybe it was time I had one. Bullshit. I rubbished the idea.

I walked into the kitchen and Marie let out a squeal of delight. 'Johnny, what took you so long this time?'

We hugged and sat down at the table and she poured me some tea before filling me in on the news. Her chatter kept me occupied, but I couldn't keep the question to myself.

'Where is everybody?'

'Resting.'

I had walked past the ward, there didn't seem to be any activity.

'It's Sunday, Johnny. You know the drill.'

I smiled. At the rehab we called it the 'sacred Sunday', a routine started by my mother, wherein the day was spent reading, praying or simply sitting in the rose garden and staring at the trees. Most patients quite enjoyed the drill, a respite from gardening, counselling and other taxing activities.

That still didn't answer my question. Where was Sera?

'Marie, I am going to the study, just ask Sera to see me after lunch.' I hoped I sounded casual.

'Sera's out.'

'Out?'

I couldn't help a raised eyebrow and got one in return.

'Just tell her to meet me when she's back.'

'That'll be late evening.'

By now, I figured Marie was bursting to tell me something.

'Out with it, Marie.'

'She's been going to Seven Seas after work and coming back late. I haven't shared a meal with her in ten days,' Marie complained.

'Ah well! She's entitled to some free time.'

Even as I said the words, the bile rose in my throat; that Sera should prefer the company of a deranged man, years younger than her, didn't go down well with me.

Leaving Marie in the kitchen, I ran up the stairs of the service apartment, which Sera shared with Marie. I had never been inside her room. It is surprising how much a person's room will tell you about aspects that never surface in public. There were books, shoes and soiled clothes, piled high, gathering dust. Not much of a homemaker, I thought. I opened the closet and was amazed to find colourful chiffon and silk dresses hanging, dresses that had not seen daylight in a very, very long time. Courtesy her sugar daddy, I suppose.

There was silver jewellery turning black in the drawers. I had never seen her wear any of it. Her nightwear was faded, worn out. I deduced that making herself attractive to her ageing husband in bed hadn't featured high on her list. There was an old snapshot of her taken at the Darling Harbour in Sydney stuck on the dresser. Her smile was as dazzling as the winter sun and she looked absolutely radiant.

In that moment, I realized I was falling in love with her. I took the picture out for closer inspection and found a note tucked under. It read, 'My fair lady, pose for me, please.' The handwriting was bold and similar to the love note on Mira's orchids. Azaan, again!

I could have killed just then, the haze of hatred crept into my head until my head ached so violently that the only option was to bang it against the wall with force. It felt good. Only pain could block pain, I had learnt the hard way.

I stuck Sera's photograph next to Mira's on the soft board in my bedroom.

Was my life also going to be like this, finding and losing

love? Lonely evenings spent staring at pictures? Just like my parents who had been caught in a pathetic compromise. Would the offspring of that compromise lead an equally miserable existence? I had to find a way to move beyond Mira.

I looked at Sera's picture. The awkward, beautiful Sera with a trunk full of clothes, books, a messy relationship and a way with patients. Could she revive me just as she had revived Mother's rose garden with her love and care?

The night seemed inviting through the window, and I walked out to soak in the starry reflection of the night sky.

I had been brooding for so long and so intensely that I did not see Sera and Azaan till they were almost upon me. Hand in hand they walked towards the rose garden, smiling. Sera, pretty in red, pointing a finger to the sky that was lit up to welcome them. Azaan looked handsome even in his work clothes. His fingers were smeared with paint and some of it was on his face too.

That they were very comfortable with each other was hard to miss; there was mischief in the air. Some would call it harmless flirting, but then harmless is not a word I could pin to Azaan.

Like fire turned low on milk that was coming to a boil, I stopped myself in time from making a fool of myself and instead said a very cool good evening to both of them.

The smile on Sera's face on hearing my voice lit up the darkness in my heart. We stared at each other for a moment before Azaan cut in.

'Back from the beach holiday, Doc? Well, no one missed you here.'

'This is private property and I'll toss you out in less than ten seconds. You are not invited in my house.'

Azaan must have increased the pressure on Sera's hand, for she yelped like a puppy and turned an unbecoming pink.

He left without uttering another word. Sera looked at his retreating back and then at me.

'He had just come to drop me.'

'To tuck you in bed?'

'What nonsense! I have just been posing for him . . . with my clothes on, Johnny. Don't give me that look.'

'What look? I don't much care for women and their boy-toys.'

'Johnny, that's absurd! There is nothing between him and me.'

'Mira used to parrot the same thing.'

'I am not Mira.'

'No, you couldn't be even if you tried.'

The moment it was out, I knew I had gone far. Her jaw dropped with the hurt, and she turned away from me. In such situations, I know what to do, but it doesn't come naturally to me. Still, I went and put an arm around her and the strangest of things happened. I felt something stir deep inside, in that vulnerable place that beats loudly when someone special is near.

It felt good. We stared at the sky. There was something between us, not the usual warring of hormones, just a sweet music that flowed from her being to mine. I suddenly felt calmer.

'Sera.'

'Hmmm?'

'Given time, could you come to love me?'

'I do.'

'Will you marry me?'

There wasn't even a pause. 'You want to sleep with me?'

'I didn't ask you to sleep with me, I asked you to marry me, Sera, marry me.'

The silence was long.

'What about you, Johnny, given time could you come to love me? I have married for the wrong reasons before.'

'What reasons?'

'To escape from my reality.'

'No one is escaping tonight.'

I carried Sera in my arms. She didn't object. She had never been in my room and, for a moment, her curiosity overrode the passion that ran like an electric charge through our skin.

She stared mesmerized at a line sketch of a bare woman astride a man with a whip in hand. The outline of full breasts and puckered nipples, darkened and shaded with charcoal against a white backdrop, made the picture very erotic.

The face in the sketch was not of much interest to me, it was the positioning of the limbs, entwined, entangled, that attracted my attention.

The sketch was a gift from my father to my mother on their wedding night; he said it would always remind her that she was on top. Not much good it did her, though. Sera asked me to put her down. I did and watched her walk up to the wall behind the ornately carved bed to look at the picture more closely.

She traced the initial 'R' at the bottom of the frame and turned to ask, 'Your father's?'

In one stride, I closed the distance between us and took

her mouth in mine. The topic of my dear father had been known to kill an erection in the past, I wasn't taking any chances. For a man it was so easy to tell a woman without telling her in so many words that he wanted her. She must have felt me growing hard; the next instance, she broke the kiss and stepped away to look into my eyes.

Much as I like to play these games, tonight I just wished to satiate the burning need for the feel of our bodies moving together. I pulled her close and crushed her in my arms. My mind, however, continued to tick-tock. I had in a moment of heat asked her to marry me, but I wasn't sure if we would be good together as lovers.

That's why the idea of arranged marriages is so strange. How can two strangers know if they would want to wake up in the same bed a few months, a year down the line?

Even lovers get bored of each other. Imagine then marrying two strangers off, and leaving them to discover if they'll be happy together. Like Robin and Daisy.

Society expects a marriage to run on commitment; how can it, when sex is one of the strongest drives in a person. If that is not satisfying between a husband and a wife, the union is bound to crumble. It sounds cynical, but it is true.

Come to think of it, Father had been the perfect victim of this sick institution called marriage. My mother knew my father had no feelings for her, but she wouldn't release him from their suffocating relationship. In that sense, they were made for each other, the spineless husband and the possessive wife.

Damn, not the train of thought I needed just then. I went to work at Sera's dress with a renewed zeal and pushed the straps of her hot pink brassier off her shoulder. It was time to look. Her athletic figured belied the fullness of her breasts.

I bit the supple flesh lightly, Sera moaned and pulled my hair. The harder I bit, the harder she pulled. It became a game until she could not bear the bites anymore.

The bite marks were red against her fair skin. I examined my handiwork with a smug look.

Which was a mistake; she pushed me on the bed and climbed on top. The look on her face was purposeful. She took the dress off and the brassiere, only a pair of black boy-shorts remained.

I smiled and said, 'All yours.'

She pinned my hands above my head and began to trace the scar with her tongue. It made me uncomfortable, but she wouldn't stop. I gave in and she kissed my eyes shut. It was bliss; her teeth nibbling my ear, her tongue, wet and slippery, ran up and down my neck. Her hands caressed the inside of my thigh, teasing, tantalizing, inches away from my crotch. When she reached my chest, she looked at me and bit my nipples as hard as she could. I would have screamed my lungs out, had she not covered my mouth with hers.

'That hurt,' I said, when we stopped to catch our breath.

'I am sure.' She smiled. Sera wasn't letting any man make love to her, she was an equal.

SERA

The New Mrs Will

If life is about tasting fulfilment in an unfulfilled existence, then who was I to question God's will? I reasoned that if I hung on long enough, Johnny would someday feel for me. Love, after all, had a strange way of creeping in on you when you least expected it to.

I walked towards the rose garden to watch the inpatients meditate in the early-morning sun. It almost always brought a sense of peace, purpose, that no matter how badly one may fall, there is always scope for getting up and walking again.

I looked at the bald pate of a patient who had been with us for six months and was to be discharged next week. His wife and children were coming to take him home. The same wife whose face he had scarred with a cigarette in a fit of drunken rage. Her crime was that she had refused to warm his evening meal at midnight. He had been full of remorse in the morning and by evening he was drinking again. It wasn't until he had hit his four-year-old daughter that the wife decided to seek outside help. It was either that or a police complaint.

The man who had walked in had low self-esteem, was

prone to violent fits and foul language at night, but turned into the perfect gentlemen in the morning.

It took Johnny and me several sessions to discover that he came from a broken household. His father had been a drinker, albeit a social one, and had no qualms about hurling abuses at his wife. After six months of intensive counselling and medication, he was ready to join the world a reformed man, a loving husband.

Each day, every patient here reinforces the belief in me that our childhood shapes us in more ways than one. In getting to know Johnny a little better every day, I find he's a sensitive man underneath the façade of cunning. Sometimes, in the wee hours of the morning, I sense him watching me sleep. He never leaves the bed without pressing his lips to my forehead. He is out of the house before me, and we greet each other as before to discuss the day's work.

Our lunch is laid out in the huge dining room where, up until now, he used to eat alone. Dinners are a cosy affair in the study by the fireplace. I have never known such happiness and it scares me to think it may all be just a dream. The two murders were forgotten, or at least relegated to the background, and a semblance of normalcy had returned since we took our vows.

Calling it a small affair would be understating it, as Marie and Sunny were our only guests and witnesses. Even Zac wasn't invited. That he was hurt at Johnny's behaviour does not surprise me. After all, he was the closest Johnny had to a friend or a brother. Could it be that the result of the paternity test may have planted a seed of doubt in Johnny's head?

In fact, Zac's demeanour towards me had changed considerably since I became Mrs Will.

The wedding was quite hush-hush on the whole. Aunt Adele was shocked beyond words and barged into Thy Will as we were sitting down for the post-wedding dinner that Marie had lovingly prepared.

'Ah, the lovebirds sharing a cosy meal.'

Her blessings were fake, like the pearls I wore. Johnny continued eating without looking up, and asked Marie to set a plate for Aunt Adele.

'Aunt Adele, now that you are here, join us for the wedding feast.'

'It was kind of sudden, Johnny, the wedding?'

'A woman as lovely as Sera is hard to resist.'

She took in my ankle length, burgundy silk dress, hair tied loosely at the nape and the dash of wine on my lips. I could tell she didn't think much of me, but that's not what she was there for.

'Have you told her that you won't be siring any children with her?' Her tone was malicious, but Johnny looked unfazed.

'I think she's aware of the issues clouding my virility, aren't you, Sera?'

'Look now, Johnny, you have angered the bride. It might do well to tame her, while you can.'

My dislike for Adele went up a notch and I couldn't bite back a retort. 'We can well manage our sex life between the two of us, Aunt Adele.'

'Oh, that was just some advice from an old woman.'

'I appreciate that, but I would rather have no one interfering in our personal life.'

A slow smile spread on Johnny's face as he watched us sparring like cats. We ate in silence.

Adele stayed put till we cut the wedding cake, which she thrust in my mouth and rubbed a dollop of whipped cream on my face. I tried to evade her but, for a woman of fifty, she was amazingly fit.

Johnny had called for a photographer and the moron chose that moment to click pictures.

So there I stood with cream on my face, tears in my eyes, Adele with a smirk on her face and a calm and composed Johnny standing a little away, distancing himself from the pair of us.

I love gifts! I knew the value of gifts. It had occurred to me that when love went out of the window, at least you had something to cling to.

And so when the brand new sedan rolled into our driveway, I jumped with joy. Johnny made the whole fuss about blindfolding me and walking me to my new car.

Such was my excitement that I kissed him in full view of the staff and the patients enjoying their mid-day break in the rose garden. We went for a drive around town, passed Aunt Adele's café, and got a sour look and a limp wave of a bony hand.

I was too happy to mind, I blew her an air kiss, and that made Johnny laugh.

There was laughter everywhere; I saw it in the very fabric of the cosmos. Childlike and vulnerable, we were in love. Johnny and I had been married a month. And it was as if a floodgate had been opened, sex was no longer just sex.

Hormones couldn't possibly explain the perpetual heady feeling, the shine in our eyes and the smiles on our lips.

I was no longer shy and would have never imagined talking dirty in bed, but every day I discovered a side of me that is wanton, brazen and quite the wild cat.

Johnny let no opportunity slip by to remind me how in the throes of passion I had once called out to him, 'Johnny, love like a man and fuck like a dog!'

I was only beginning to discover the dynamics of a man–woman relationship. And that the scriptures weren't lying when they talked about a spiritual awakening in the union of two bodies. There was a subtle plane beyond gratification that could only be reached when you didn't simply mate, you celebrated. And there was plenty to celebrate between Johnny and me. The memory of a certain celebration made me smile.

In my quiet moments, I thought of Mira. How different life would have been had she been around. I would still be living in the outhouse, pining for Johnny, while she kept him wrapped around her little finger.

Going from being a mere employee to the mistress of Thy Will, it all seemed like a dream sometimes. Yet, here I was blossoming right in front of everyone's curious eyes.

Azaan thought so too, for I often found him looking at me curiously. He never brought up that kiss we had shared at Adam's Edge, though. The equation was one of easy camaraderie and neither of us wished to jeopardize it. He continued to flirt with me the way he used to. I didn't mind – 'I can handle spoilt brats' is what I told Johnny.

His painting was near completion. The easel, the canvas, the colour palate, the strokes across the canvas, our conversation, all seemed so familiar now; I missed my evenings with him.

It was only lately that I had begun to feel comfortable enough with him to talk about my stifled upbringing, my sham of a first marriage and my oh-so-wonderful new lease of life with Johnny. Azaan rarely ever interrupted, encouraging me to talk as much as I want. Most days my love for Johnny was difficult to contain and, like a child eager to tell, I overloaded Azaan with stories of Johnny's escapades.

He didn't seem to mind and gave me an affectionate nod from behind the canvas every now and then. Needless to say, I was not allowed to see how the painting was shaping up. An hour every day seemed to fly by, and soon I was back in Johnny's arms.

That day was no different, except that Azaan came and stood behind me.

He took the pin out of my hair and arranged the hair around my shoulders. Having done that he came and sat close by.

'You seem happy, Sera, not the tightly coiled woman I kissed at Adam's Edge.'

I found the proximity disturbing, not in a threatening sort of way, but there was this element of want in it.

'You know your painting is so different from what I had set out to capture.'

'Different?'

'Reeks disgustingly of love,' he joked.

'That's a good thing then.'

'I would hate to see you get hurt like he hurt her.'

'No one's hurting anybody, Azaan.'

'Mira did end up dead with a child in her belly.'

'It wasn't Johnny's! He can't . . .' I stopped myself in time.

'When I look at you, Sera, I am reminded of her. During

her last days, she looked just like you, very much in love. She had come to visit me. Johnny had asked her to marry him, she showed me the ring.'

'Stop!' I didn't want to hear anymore.

'Let me finish, Sera.'

'Why are you telling me all this now? I am married to him, remember?' I showed him the rock on my finger. His eyes dilated in recognition.

'Son-of-a-bitch, it's the same ring he gave Mira!'

'Well, why buy another ring if you already have one?' I tried to laugh it off. Even as I was making up this excuse, the coldness in my heart was beginning to spread all over.

'She had come to inform me of her decision to marry Johnny, out of sheer respect for her betrothal to me.'

'You knew about the baby?'

'No.' The denial didn't ring true.

'She wanted me to convince Uncle Kermani to let her marry an outsider. I was so angry I called her names. That's the last time I saw her.'

'It wasn't your fault.'

'No, it was Johnny's. Not even three months of her death and the bastard has already put her ring on your finger.'

I turned the ring around my finger. The stone had lost its charm.

We sat there a long time. Our twisted lives entangled some more by the emotions that ran deep under the surface. Mira's death had affected Azaan more deeply than he cared to admit.

Tears floated in Azaan's eyes and his breathing became uneven. He made a superhuman effort to remain in control. Men are not supposed to cry. I wish they could; it would ease their pain and much of the anguish their pent-up emotions caused others. If only they would let go once in a while.

I suddenly felt like the world was a lonely place. Togetherness was an illusion; for some, it lasted a little longer than for others. For Azaan, it was worse. The bipolar disorder he suffered from caused acute mood swings. He didn't need another soul to make him miserable.

But I could comfort him, couldn't I? Holding him close brought a sense of calm. Human touch was a wonderful thing. Azaan smiled and hugged me back.

But that moment was not without the uncanny feeling that we were being watched. I could not have anticipated that my loving husband would arrive to pick me up at precisely that moment and watch the little scene.

I came to know of it much later and by then there was no point in trying to explain why I was in Azaan's arms.

Uncle Robin

Married life suits Johnny terribly well. He no longer had a reason to sit in his glass cabin, chatting with patients longer than necessary. The files and bills were signed almost immediately, no reminders required. But pinning down Johnny is a tough task. After three weeks of trying to speak to him alone, I had come to the conclusion that he was avoiding me.

He was probably feeling guilty about not inviting his little brother to the wedding. Or the result of the paternity test had really psyched him.

But if that were the case, I wouldn't have been alive. Johnny doesn't possess the thing they call conscience and would have happily slit my throat. Even as a child, he was quick to mark things as his own. He wasn't really sold on the idea of sharing; his toys and mine were separate. He would demand the most expensive toys to be bought for him, while I was happy if mother gifted me a comic book.

If he was angry with me, unlike other children who fight with their siblings, Johnny simply gave me the silent treatment. I was always trying to please him, just like I spent my life trying to please Adele.

It was only much later that I figured both Adele and Johnny were cut out from the same fabric, both born manipulators.

So, there had to be a solid reason for Johnny to avoid me, something definitely substantial. My own reason for seeking him out wasn't too altruistic either. I was conducting a personal inquiry into the missing morphine boxes. The question was no longer who had taken them. Rather, would the killer use the remaining 200 mg to commit another murder?

I saw Johnny heading for his rounds. I ran after him, nabbed and pressed his body against the wall, a game we used to play as kids.

'Hey, Zac, my bro, we aren't very civilized this morning. Come, let's have a cup of coffee.'

'I thought you would never ask.' He put his arms around me and we went to his cabin.

'Johnny, two boxes of morphine are unaccounted for. You wouldn't know anything about it, by any chance?'

'Sunny did mention something along those lines. No, we haven't had any need of using morphine here and certainly not 400 mg of it. This is a rehab, not a trauma centre, you know that.'

Two things were not right: one, Johnny didn't seem concerned; two, the news didn't fluster him. His eyes locked with mine. 'So what do you want me to do, Zac?'

'All I want to know is, are we going to tell Officer Ray about it, or do we sit tight?'

'Hmm, you have posed a serious question here, little brother.'

I waited patiently for Johnny to say something. When he didn't, I unleashed my fury on him.

'Do you even realize what this means, Johnny? It means that somebody who has access to Thy Will killed Mira and has enough morphine on him to commit another murder.'

Johnny was lost in thought and when he spoke his words chilled the warm flesh on my bones.

'Yes, Officer Ray needs to be informed. We don't want the same fate for Sera now, do we?'

The inspector at the local police station was miffed that I asked for Officer Ray and not him. In a very curt voice, he told me that Ray had gone back to town. I politely requested him to give me a number where I could reach him.

He put me on hold for what seemed like an eternity and came back with a number. No thank you was required; he had put the receiver down.

I often think people are discourteous to me because of my illegitimate status, which was common knowledge. Or maybe it had to do with my paranoia about being a bastard.

I called Officer Ray on his direct line. A bored hello came through. Time to chase the policeman's boredom away, I thought. In retrospect, I should have done no such thing. But not letting sleeping dogs lie is an old habit of the Wills and we often pay for it with blood.

'Interesting, that you should be sitting on this information for so long.'

'There wasn't any point in raising the alarm if Sera and Johnny had used the morphine on the patients.'

'Why tell me now?'

'It's obvious that the killer is someone closely associated with Thy Will.'

'How about you, Zac, could you have . . .?'

'Sure, arrest me,' I snapped.

'Maybe I will.'

Great! The asshole suspected me of stealing the morphine. I wish I had simply left the ball in Johnny's court. Sera was, after all, Johnny's wife and he could very well take care of her. Or could he? My mind went back to the fateful night when Thy Will had been this close to burning. My father, Uncle Robin to me in those days, had a fondness for the bastard son. His own son, Johnny, spoke to him with such disrespect that it brought tears to the old man's eyes. He would inquire often how I was doing at school. It was another thing that he never remembered about the basketball match I won, the math test I failed or which class I studied in.

A repeat telecast of the same questions was done at frequent intervals. The alcohol had dimmed his cognitive functions to such an extent that he sometimes mistook day for night and Marie for his wife.

Most nights he fell down and remained on the floor till someone came and picked him up. Ours was a very sad household. After a while, Johnny was fed up of the night routine and would often scold me for picking him from the floor.

He would say, 'Zac, let the drunkard be. I am done cleaning up his mess. Let him lie in his own vomit.' And so he did many evenings.

On one particular evening, Uncle Robin was sprawled on the floor, drooling and crying out for help. As I went close, he begged me to pick him up and take him to the study. At his request, I got his glass of favourite whisky and a packet of Navy Cuts. He patted my hand and asked me to sit.

'Zac, you are no less than anybody.'

To avoid his gaze I began to draw a sketch of him on a rough sheet on his desk. Halfway through, he snatched it from my hand and exclaimed loudly, 'My boy can draw!' I wanted to say, so can Johnny. 'Come on, draw, finish it, let's see how much talent you got.'

I hesitated, but I finished it nevertheless.

'Excellent detailing, Zac. Maybe you can be a famous cartoonist like me someday, huh?'

'Papa, the only thing you are famous for in the whole of Monele is living on my mother's money, whom you also happened to kill,' Johnny piped in from the doorway.

I feared a scene between father and son and asked Johnny to hold his tongue.

There was no stopping Johnny, he was furious and pushed me out of the study saying, 'You stay out of it, Zac, it's between him and me.' With that, he turned back to his father. 'You are a loser and not fit enough to live among civilized, educated people!'

Uncle Robin just closed his eyes and tried to block the drama unfolding in front of him.

'Don't speak to me like that, I am your father.'

'Do me a favour then, drop dead.'

He did.

That evening was the last I ever saw of Uncle Robin. His shame, his drink and a smouldering cigarette became the end of him. Johnny never shed a tear.

He was probably in that room watching Uncle Robin burn, screaming for help, while he added final touches to the sketch I had left half finished.

Johnny, the fat little boy, was cold-blooded; Johnny, the grown man, was ruthless.

Marie

The Python's Youth

The aroma of the freshly brewed coffee from the tray I was carrying wafted to the master bedroom. Johnny had left ten minutes ago, asking me to take coffee for Sera.

After the second knock, I pushed the door open and peeped inside. She was neither on the bed nor in the balcony, which could only mean she was in the bathroom. I kept the cup by her sidetable and was about to leave when the sound of Sera throwing up came from behind the bathroom door. Putting my head to the door I asked, 'Are you alright, Sera?'

No response.

'Sera, are you okay?'

The door opened and Sera came out, pressing a towel to her forehead.

'I am fine, something must not have agreed with my stomach, a stale dish maybe.'

'But everything I cook is fresh!'

'Oh no, Marie, I didn't mean here. Something I must have eaten at Seven Seas; they usually serve quite a few delicacies, which I find hard to resist after sitting still for hours.'

'These fancy places are all the same, you be careful, Sera. We don't want you falling ill before your wedding bash.'

'I am not stealing the limelight, Marie; the party is to celebrate Johnny's thirty-fourth birthday. There is shopping to be done and invites to be sent out.'

'The week has just begun. I'll make a list of groceries, beverages and decorations and ask Zac to fetch them. We'll finish all preparations in good time.'

'Oh, Marie, what would I do without you!'

'My only concern is that some of the rooms have not been aired for years. Maybe Johnny can hire some temporary help.'

'I'll help you; in fact, I would love to open some old boxes myself, Marie.'

'First you get better, dear. Throwing up every morning shouldn't become a routine.'

I left her to have coffee in peace and realized I had said the wrong thing. Morning sickness comes with carrying a child, something she would never experience. I felt bad for her. An old spinster like me probably knew more than anyone else about the void that came with not being a mother. My need had been largely filled by Johnny and Zac, the tales of their childhood are many. Johnny was always my favourite; the sadness in his keen eyes was hard to miss even when he was just a child. It was such a shame that there would never be a Johnny junior playing in the yard.

This house has seen so much, I wondered what else the good Lord had planned for us. A sigh escaped my weary form as I piled the dishes in the kitchen sink.

'The new mistress keeping you on your toes, Marie?'

'Adele.'

'You should retire now.' With a smile, I offered her coffee but she waved it away.

'Not good for my ulcers.'

'Since when did you have ulcers, Adele?'

'Age is catching up, Marie.'

'Ah! You needn't worry about old age; you'll probably outlive all of us,' I said with a hint of sarcasm.

She laughed in her high-pitched musical way and enquired how the newlyweds were doing. I wanted to tell her they were happy and much in love, but I feared her black tongue and mumbled a lame okay.

'Sera, up or spending the day lazing in bed?'

'She's not feeling too well this morning, been throwing up.'

Adele's pallor changed to an unhealthy yellow. 'Does Johnny know?'

'Know what?'

'Never mind.'

Adele's behaviour, even in her younger days, was no less bizarre. She was always sneaking about the house and listening outside doors. But that had not always been the case. Adele had not only been beautiful, but brilliant too. Her father doted on her and there were reasons to justify it. She had won a gold medal in her college and had got offers from prestigious universities.

That summer she was waiting out, there were long family discussions as to which university would best groom her academic career.

As fate would have it, Grandpa Will had suffered a massive coronary and barely survived. Daisy, who had been recently married, rushed back home from Ooty with her famous cartoonist husband to look after her father.

While Daisy looked after the sick and needy father, Adele spent much of her time discussing her love of books, politics and art with her brother-in-law.

Grandpa Will never did recover completely, and the doctors gave him only a year to live. Daisy and Robin stayed back.

Summer passed and winter came, but Adele did not go to town to pursue higher studies. She was in love.

Of course, there was guilt, plenty of it, in the beginning. I would hear her weeping in the balcony many a night. But a heart that loves knows not sin; it only beats for the other.

How time flies! Here Adele was, sapped of the vitality that had once made her a woman of great beauty and charm.

Out of curiosity I asked, 'What brings you to this part of the house, Adele? You rarely come here.'

'Oh, I am just checking what all changes could be made in the kitchen when Zac finally moves in.'

I stood rooted to the spot as if she had struck me. She ran her hand by the counter, picked up an old pan and said, 'Some of this stuff is prehistoric and needs to go.' With that she dropped the pan on the floor.

'Zac moving in?' I gulped.

'Why, Marie, won't you cook meals for my son?'

I could only stare at her. Deranged was the only word in my limited vocabulary that fit Adele. She was losing it, I was certain. But this was not to be the end of my woes, the day was far from over.

Sera and Johnny finished their supper and I started clearing the plates from the study. Many times during the evening, I wanted to tell Johnny that the old python was up to no good, but he seemed so happy, I didn't want even a shadow of alarm or pain to mar his happiness.

I waited for Sera to leave. Usually, Johnny finished his work as he smoked a cigar and called it a day an hour after dinner. I went in again, carrying a new flavour of mouth freshener for Johnny to taste, as an excuse to get his attention.

Johnny was not fooled. 'Yes, Marie, you have been hovering around all evening, what is it?'

I opened my mouth, but the blood-curdling scream that came out was not mine. Johnny was out of his chair in a second. I wobbled after him. The screams were now interspersed with sobs. I heard Johnny shouting loudly.

'Who is there? Who is there?'

Sera was crying uncontrollably, pointing to the bathroom window.

He opened the window and jumped out. 'There is no one here, Sera, come, look.'

'No, no, Johnny! He was watching me . . .' she cried, unable to stop the tears from falling. 'There was a face pressed to the window . . .' And she broke down again.

It was a huge window of glazed glass. Johnny closed the window from outside and pressed his face against the glass. It was a chilling sight, brown skin flattened against white glass, and dark, furtive eyes like that of a sly animal. Sera screamed again.

'Johnny, he was right there, just like that.'

'Did you recognize him?'

'No, I was so scared, so scared,' she wailed.

He took her in his arms and held her tight and slowly steered her towards the window. She resisted, paralysed with fear, eyes squeezed shut.

'Darling, open your eyes, see for yourself, you can't see anything from the outside. The bastard couldn't see anything. Whoever it was, was just trying to scare you.'

Oh, he had done a thorough job of that. She was hysterical,

incapable of speaking and Johnny's lips were a tight line. Thy Will had an old guard who kept a watch at the building, but security at the main house had never been any issue. There was only a low boundary wall around the building that wouldn't keep someone out if they were determined to enter.

It could be anyone from the staff. The big question was, why would someone want to scare Sera in the first place?

Picture in a Frame

The first flush of love is a delight to capture on canvas, like the sun blushing orange. The oil colours were bringing the sketch out nicely.

The fullness of the lips painted red was a stroke of genius, I marvelled. The fact that I had kissed those lips brought them especially alive for me. It was the painting of a woman much in love. Therein lay the problem. She was in love with the wrong man. A man I hated.

The fifty-page police report on Mira's murder lay in Uncle Kermani's study, and I had read it a hundred times. Every damn interview, case finding, the evidence was there to see. It began with Johnny's claim of being parked outside Mira's apartment. He claimed her door was locked, while in reality the neighbours found the door open from the inside.

Then there was the sketch, the butcher's knife and the orchids. The orchids that I had sent to apologize for my behaviour. But there was no mention of a note in the report, a note so suggestive it would have definitely played on Officer Ray's mind.

A passion flower,
Sweet to taste, Silk to feel,
Layer by layer . . . heaven to peel.

It would have pushed any sane man to the edge and Johnny was far from sane. I was sure that I was in some way responsible for Mira's death.

The report also mentioned that though the DNA of the baby was a forty per cent match, Johnny was sterile. Some childhood injury had left him infertile.

The bastard couldn't be fucking sterile, he was fooling the police. Another shocking footnote in Officer Ray's unintelligible handwriting made me sit up and take note. It stated that there is a possibility that Johnny and Zac are half brothers; that would explain the DNA match despite Johnny's sterility. Zac could very well then be the father of the unborn child. I had known Mira to be promiscuous, but not since the time she had been with Johnny; she had left that lifestyle behind.

I gave the Zac–Mira angle some more thought. Zac was attractive, in a beefy, mean kind of way. What did Mira like? I didn't know anymore. We knew that we were to be married someday, that's what Uncle Kermani had intended for us all along. Neither Mira nor I had a problem with that until she met Johnny, or was it Zac? Could Johnny have come to know of Mira's fling with Zac, and in a fit of rage punished Mira for cheating on him?

Johnny could kill, the story about him torching his father in his youth was repeated often at the local bars. Hearsay wasn't always untrue.

The report also had some disturbing things to say about

Sera's first marriage and made references to a morphine overdose. The beautiful Sera didn't seem so appealing anymore. She was, after all, quick to slip Mira's engagement ring onto her finger. Could the current Mrs Johnny Will have eliminated the competition? Women can never be trusted. And certainly not Johnny's woman. The bastard had to be taught a lesson.

I looked at her painting with a new eye, erased all signs of the innocence in those vulnerable eyes and started all over again.

SERA

The Whole Truth

The chandelier hung from the high ceiling, the cleaning of which seemed an arduous task, but it had to be done. The first guest would arrive in less than six hours from now. I had invited some old patients who held Johnny in high regard. It was going to be a cosy affair, family, friends and well-wishers to ring in Johnny's thirty-fourth birthday.

I had taken the day off to help Marie in the house. I finished dusting the large living room and placed freshly plucked flowers from the garden in the antique flower vase. I took a moment to inspect my handiwork and liked what I saw. A mental pat on the back and I decided to wash the dust off my hands.

Entering the bathroom made me uneasy, but I quelled the feeling with a determined stride and walked to the basin. Since the night I had seen that face in the window, I felt violated. The sound of my own screams haunted my dreams.

I had hoped Marie wouldn't tell anybody about the night's incident, but she did, and that too to my greatest well-wisher, Adele.

'You were frightened, Sera?'

'Terribly.'

'Did you see who it was?'

'No, I didn't.'

'What were you up to when you saw the face in the window?'

'Brushing my teeth,' I lied.

'No show time, huh? Good, wouldn't want the bastard to see you changing clothes.'

Adele laughed. Her knowing eyes full of malice looked back at me. I had hoped to strike her off the guest list and had even spoken to Johnny about it, but was surprised to find him jump to her defence.

'I don't much care for her but I don't want to offend Zac. Besides, the whole town will talk about how we have been neglecting the old, frail aunt.'

'She isn't frail! I get such bad vibes from her. I don't know why she even comes here.'

'She never came to see me in all these years, I guess she likes you,' he said dryly and went back to work.

Marie's voice called out to me. We were to dig out cutlery and fine china from the basement.

'Coming, Marie.'

I was still annoyed with Marie for telling Adele about the bathroom incident.

'Marie, in the future, whatever goes on in the house must remain in the house.'

Marie was taken aback by my curt tone and she replied equally curtly, 'Thy Will is my house, too. You have not been married a month and you are questioning my loyalty to this house?'

'What was the need to tell Adele about that incident at my window?'

'I didn't tell her anything.' With that she stomped out.

If Marie had not told Adele, how did Adele know I was changing clothes and not brushing my teeth?

I regretted speaking to Marie like that. Not knowing what to do, I just stood there, dejected. She came from behind and patted my head. I wanted to apologize, but she didn't let me and guided me to the staircase. We walked down the staircase silently, but I knew that Marie had found it in her large heart to forgive me. I felt my tense muscles relax and looked forward to our work in the basement.

The basement was not some messy space where things were dumped. Everything was neatly stacked. Trunks full of clothes, tapestry, quilts and satin covers were on one side, wooden articles, old toys, books and albums in another corner.

There was a handmade cradle made of rubberwood, a 'J' craved on its side. I rocked it gently and it made a creaking sound that made Marie say, 'That was Johnny's. Robin made it for him before he was born.'

Robin must have loved his son very much to have spent hours carving a cradle out of wood. I had not once heard Johnny take his father's name.

A strange family this was. Still, I was so enamoured by the old-world charm that I left Marie to the task of cleaning and went about finding my way around the basement. I pulled out an old wedding album that read 'Daisy weds Robin'. Looking at his father's pictures, one could tell where Johnny got his good looks from. But Robin was well-built, pretty much like Zac. Johnny had inherited the lean frame from his mother. Daisy had a pretty smile and looked enchanting in her wedding dress. On her finger shone the diamond that I now wore on mine.

Relief washed over me and I thanked God for leading me to Daisy. I had not been able to muster up the courage to question Johnny about the ring since Azaan had planted that seed of doubt in my head. I had the answer now. The ring was a family heirloom that the mother would want her son's bride to have.

I felt a certain kinship to Daisy even though she was long dead. I looked around for some more personal treasures and found a broken chest with the letter D carved on it.

It was crammed with broken pieces of fake jewellery, hairpins, a passbook and some old letters. I took the letters out; they were yellow with age. Each one had been written in a neat handwriting and began with 'my dear Robin', all except one.

The bold, cursive 'darling' caught my attention.

> Darling Robin,
>
> My days pass but evenings barely crawl. I go for walks alone and can't wait for you to return from your assignment. There is much to tell.
>
> Today, Zac came home crying. The children in his class have learnt a new word, 'bastard', and for obvious reasons, they chose to address your son by that name. I am tired of people treating us as filth and I won't have my son pay the price of our misdeeds.
>
> Won't you free us from this life of misery?
>
> Maybe Daisy will find it in her heart to accept Zac and me. If only you would take a stand and accept us as your own.
>
> Robin, I am tired of this charade. So what if we won't have money and a grand house like Thy Will

to live in? We'll have each other. We'll build our own place slowly . . . I feel so deeply for you and I know in my heart that you do too. You do, don't you?

Forever yours,
Adele

I reread the letter. Much as I felt bad for Daisy to have had her world devastated by this note, it was Adele's words that played on my mind.

'Won't you free us from this life of misery?'

So, Johnny and Zac were indeed half-brothers and that unborn baby could be Zac's. The neglect Zac received as a child, being the illegitimate son and growing up with no money despite the Wills being a wealthy family, must be a source of great bitterness. I was scared of Zac.

And then there is Adele.

I tried to picture her as a young woman in love with a man, bearing his child and braving the wrath of the family. A pretty hellish life for an unwedded mother of twenty-two. I wondered what I would have done in her shoes.

What amazed me was Robin's ability to father a child, but his inability to take responsibility for the mother and son. Inability, a fascinating word if one thinks about it, different from incapable. For the first time I admitted to myself that Johnny's twisted ideals were deep-rooted and he might never be the man I could look up to.

His childhood had robbed him of one of the greatest gifts parents give to their children, that of warmth and values . . . morals. Maybe it's a good thing then that we won't be having any children. No children? The truth of my married life was beginning to sink in.

Last-minute panic had gripped Marie in the kitchen. The icing on the three-tier cake had not settled. Marie had very beautifully crafted a dancing couple and the current crisis was that the male dancer's head was melting slowly because of the heat. She rushed to fix his hair and shove the cake in the fridge.

People had started arriving. Marie shooed me out of the kitchen to get dressed.

I quickly wrapped a blue chiffon sari around my waist and pinned a white flower behind my ear. I used the blusher liberally to highlight my cheeks and a pencil to shape my brows into an arch. The overall effect was dazzling. I should catch my husband's eye tonight.

Our honeymoon was more or less over. Johnny was preoccupied with work and if I had not been so busy with the party preparations, I would have noticed the coolness in his manner towards me. I laid Johnny's black suit on the bed and went to look for him. As I neared his cabin in the facility, the sound of raised voices carried well into the corridor. It was Officer Ray, and he was certainly not here to wish Johnny a happy birthday.

'You could have taken it.'

'Well, so could have Sera and Zac himself.'

What could I have taken that Johnny mentioned with such confidence? I eavesdropped.

'Your wife does seem to have an interesting history.'

'She does?'

'Her first husband had overdosed on morphine and was just about saved in time but the old fella had a stroke. I bet you didn't know that.'

There was silence.

'How about the story of her penniless state, and that she wasn't really married to him? She was just living off him; with you she got lucky, I guess.'

'Hold your tongue, Officer, that's my wife you are talking about. She's told me every goddamn thing there is to know.'

I hadn't. Quietly, I backtracked into our bedroom and sat down to weigh my options.

The Merry Crowd

All the players were here.

Zac with Anna, Kermani with Azaan and Adele coughing all over Marie.

The person I was delighted to see was Mrs Baines. She looked out of place, though much in control of herself, unlike the last time I had seen her. I nursed my drink and observed the people gathered around Johnny.

A man in a cowboy hat was chatting with Johnny. He was loud enough to be heard by all.

'You couldn't have chosen better, Johnny. Sera has blossomed into a rare beauty. I could cast her in my film.'

'You certainly can, Mr Sarkar. Sera has many hidden talents that I am only beginning to discover.'

Sera calmly sipped her wine, looking disinterested.

Azaan signalled her with his eyes as if seeking permission to approach her in public view. She must have answered in the affirmative, for Azaan walked towards Sera, clutching a gift-wrapped package in his hands.

Sera met him midway. He gave her the present.

The blush on Sera's face rose high. It was after all her husband's day to receive gifts.

Johnny and every other eye in the room watched Sera unwrap the gift. It seemed like a movie adaptation of an Agatha Christie novel, the setting, the suspects and I, the lone investigator. Sera had drunk deeply of her wine before she attacked the wrapper. The packaging wouldn't come off easily. When it did, it revealed a canvas. Sera's sharp intake of breath echoed in the room.

Johnny marched forward and snatched it out of her hand. The circle of people inched closer to have a look. A bare back painted artistically and the skin shone in places where the shadow fell. The woman in the painting lay on her stomach, a tantalizing silhouette of her full breast, her eyes a chalice full of passion. Her long hair trailed behind. The similarity between the picture and Sera was hard to ignore.

Azaan had used shades of brown and black, yet the painting looked so full of life. It was probably the blood red he had used liberally to paint the lips.

'A marvellous bedroom piece,' said Anna, hanging onto Zac's arm.

The canvas would have broken under the pressure Johnny applied to it, so Zac took it out of his hand. That Sera looked stunned is an understatement. She probably wasn't expecting Azaan to make this painting public.

The awkward moment stretched until the housekeeper wheeled the cake in. Zac took charge and invited everyone for the cake-cutting. The note of false gaiety in the air became louder with each moment as the birthday song was sung. Sera now looked less shaken, more drunk.

Johnny did not blow at the candle, he simply plucked it out. The first piece he put into Marie's mouth as Sera looked on. The second one went into his mouth. Embarrassed, Sera looked away. Everyone congratulated Johnny, while Marie showed the cake around.

Sera stalked out. I followed her.

She went up to the terrace and sat looking at the moon. The yellow orb stared back and she began to hum sorrowfully. I saw Johnny coming her way. I was quick to hide behind the door, curious to know if a possessive lover also made for a jealous husband.

'Come back to the party.'

She didn't bat an eyelid.

'Look at me when I am talking to you, Sera. If you wanted to sleep around, why marry me?'

'He's no one to me, Johnny! Nobody!'

'Just like a kiss one would share with a nobody at Adam's Edge?'

'Ah, Adele, of course,' Sera mocked. 'Johnny, she's a pathological liar.'

'Or maybe you are? You did hug him, didn't you?'

Sera was lost for a moment.

'No!' she lied boldly.

'Really, you lying, scheming woman. I had come to pick you up that evening. Unfortunately, I changed my plans in view of the warm embrace you were exchanging with your lover.'

Sera's glance was full of hurt.

'Come back to the party. You are not making a fool of me in front of my guests.'

Sera started to hum.

'Look at me when I am talking to you, Sera.'

She jammed her fingers in her ears to block his voice. Her humming became louder and so did Johnny's discomfort.

'Where did you hear that?' he asked quietly, deathly pale.

Sera's voice grew stronger.

'Shut up, Sera!' Johnny screamed in anger.

Her voice rang out clear in the silent night.

'Johnny had a little rabbit,
Mira had a fucking habit,
Rabbit died, Mira lied, Johnny cried.'

Johnny clamped her mouth shut and would have probably suffocated her to death if Sera hadn't whimpered and struggled to free herself rather violently.

'Who told you about this? Zac? Adele? I swear I'll kill you, tell me!'

A scared Sera spoke up. 'I heard Azaan saying it when he was locked up!'

'Your toy-boy doesn't know anything about my childhood. Nobody knows!' he thundered.

'Was it Zac? Are you sleeping with him, like Mira was?' Johnny yelled at Sera. She began to cry.

I left them both to their misery and went in search of Azaan. The smug look on his face told me he had accomplished what he had come for – to steal Johnny's wife, not literally though. I recited the rhyme to Azaan. The tune was quite catchy, he began to hum with me.

'I did come across it somewhere.'

'Where?'

'The general had a journal at the rehab that he used to keep close to his heart.'

I remembered the torn pages of that red bound journal I had found in the general's room.

'Did you read it?' I asked excitedly.

'Oh, no, it was mostly full of poetic nonsense. I browsed through it once and this was the only rhyme I could make sense of,' he grumbled.

How did the general know of a childhood incident that nobody knew about, except the people involved in it? Zac didn't seem the type to tell tales, but it felt right up Adele's alley to entertain the general in her café with stories of Johnny's misfortune. It could mean that the general was quite close to Adele, contrary to her claim of the general being just another customer. An image of the bottle of Sexanoil flashed in my mind. Maybe it was Adele who the general was keen on impressing. And what about the pages torn from the journal? There must be something in that journal that could incriminate the killer, otherwise why bother tearing them? I had to find the missing pages at all cost, if they had not been destroyed already.

The 'Closed' sign hung outside the café. I decided to wait for Adele to come around to open the shop. To kill time, I went into the neighbouring café to grab a bite. By now, the townsfolk knew that 'Bada Sahib' had been hovering around in the hope of solving the two murders, rather unsuccessfully. I placed my order.

Over sandwiches and strawberry shake (an awfully frothy, pink, milky concoction), I asked the owner if he had any idea what time Café Aspen was likely to open.

'Can't say, Sahib. Lately, she opens it late in the afternoon and sometimes she doesn't open at all. She doesn't need business like I do. Customers are always flocking to her café. It's good her shutter is down, that way people come to my restaurant.' Talkative fellow, I thought, not that I minded, any company was better than having lunch alone.

'Any idea why the shutter is down?'

'The other day I needed change and I went in to get some, her eyes looked feverish and she was coughing terribly into her handkerchief.'

'The weather is changing; already winter is a month late this year,' I said conversationally.

'Sahib, there was blood on the handkerchief, lots of it.'

'You didn't ask what's wrong?'

'She said, her tooth had been extracted.'

'That explains it then,' I said, sucking at the straw, finishing the last of the strawberry shake. Somehow, the handkerchief bothered me.

Adele Will had become an irritation in the eye. I had to take the irritant out to focus on the real case. I made my way to her house. It was a rundown place, much in need of repair. Adele's grievance against Johnny made sense if one compared the two houses the aunt and the nephew lived in. And what of Zac? He must surely nurse a grudge against the half-brother who had it all: name, money and respect, while he and his mother rotted away in this shabby house.

I pressed the buzzer twice, thrice, but there was no movement in the house.

Zac, I presumed, was at the rehab, but where was Adele if not home?

I went around the house, peeped in from the back door, but there was no one in the house. I went in through the back door. To my surprise, it was spic and span inside. Some of the furniture seemed to have been brought in from the main house.

Adele was a homemaker. The house smelt of freshly baked bread, there were no dirty utensils in the sink. The living room was neat and sparsely decorated. The small dining table had an assortment of homemade jams and pickles.

I had not imagined Adele Will to be a woman who took pride in her house. The first room was Zac's, the bed was ornately carved and probably the same bed he had been sleeping in as a child. It wasn't a spacious room, but a single bed left enough space to move about freely. Clothes hung neatly and his books were piled high by the bedside. The man liked to read the likes of Gandhi, Nehru and Vivekananda. Interesting.

His study table had some files, which had Thy Will written on them, mainly consisting of expenses and account statements. I leafed through some and found nothing of any interest.

Adele's room was next. Again, a single bed; it seemed like the mother and son had similar tastes. Her wardrobe was meagre, a few black dresses, sandals and out-of-fashion hats from the yesteryears. There was a framed photo of a younger Zac with Johnny, whose face had surely been scratched out by Adele's claws. A threadbare Bible lay on the dresser, the only item gathering dust in the otherwise neat and tidy room. I found it surprising that the good Lord did not get any of Adele's attention.

I was fascinated by its leather binding, it seemed to be very old, a collector's item. My curiosity made me open the Bible, the ink on the yellow pages had faded, but the verses had not lost their meaning with time.

The failing of men is hard to define,
Their feelings even worse,
They come and go,
Just as a sneeze runs down the nose,
To be wiped in a flash of a movement . . . gone,
Their touch so fake,
That for donkey's years they'll fool their women,
Believing that they love.

This was definitely written in the loving memory of Robin.

The poet in me longed to dwell on the implication of these lines, but time was running out. Reluctantly, I tossed the Bible back and it missed the dresser, falling to the ground. A sound akin to metal or a coin hitting the floor rang out.

I looked all around and found that an old key had tumbled out. I bent to retrieve it and saw the black trunk underneath Adele's bed. It had a silver lock. I was holding a silver key. Should I push my luck? I checked my watch; I had already been in the house for fifteen minutes and it would be very awkward if someone were to walk in. Without a search warrant, I shouldn't have been doing the things I was doing. I quickly unlocked the trunk. It was full of yeasty-smelling files and paper. There was a pile of rough sheets, sketches, cartoons all signed with the initial 'R'. Adele's trunk, like her heart, was filled with Robin and his memorabilia. I pulled the pile out, hoping to find an old love letter. It wasn't relevant to the case, but it would satisfy my morbid curiosity about their relationship.

The more curious I got, the more frantically I searched and it was then that I hit the jackpot, twice in a row. I held in my hand a medical report that stated Adele was suffering from bone metastatic cancer in its third stage. The second report confirmed Mira's pregnancy. Both reports were from the same clinic in town.

What was Mira's report doing in Adele's trunk? I sifted through the stuff and found a note addressed to Mira, the kind you would attach with flowers . . . orchids.

I stuffed the note in my pocket, reports in the back of my trousers and dumped everything back in the trunk. As I crossed the living room, something came over me and I decided to rummage through the dustbin in the kitchen. There it was, an empty 20-mg ampoule of morphine. With impatient hands, I drove back to the guesthouse and dialled the clinic's number. A curt voice on the phone informed me that they do not give out confidential information on the phone. A drive to town meant wasting precious time, which I did not have.

I demanded to speak to the doctor whose signature was on both the reports. The police are rarely kept holding the line and the lady doctor was quick to answer all my queries.

'I have a six-month-old report that confirms the pregnancy of Mira Kermani.'

'Whose? We handle a lot of cases at the clinic.'

'Never mind.'

Mira was smart to have had her test done outside town where no one knew her.

'What about Adele Will? She's a patient of yours suffering from cancer.'

'I remember Adele, Officer, she's not doing too well.'

'Chemotherapy?'

'No, she refused chemo.'

'Is it because the treatment is quite painful?'

'Not any more painful than the cancer that has spread to her bones. Most patients can't bear the excruciating pain in the third stage.'

How was Adele managing then?

'Would morphine help?'

'Certainly, Officer. It did when we started, but it's an addictive drug and we don't prescribe it on a regular basis.' The ampoule in the dustbin proved otherwise. Then who was supplying morphine to Adele? Zac? But it was Zac who had brought to my attention the fact that there was a discrepancy in the rehab records. It would be very foolish of him to steal and then implicate himself. Adele's use of morphine explained the missing boxes from the rehab. How did Adele get access to them then?

One box had been used to drain the life out of Mira's slender body, while the other was helping Adele breathe easy. Adele had little time to live and enough morphine supply to kill Mira and frame Johnny. All in the best interest of her son, Zac Will. The motive at this point seemed simple; she wanted Zac to inherit Thy Will. But something was amiss.

The dots were beginning to connect. But why would Mira's pregnancy bother Adele? If she wanted Zac to inherit Thy Will, it made more sense to kill Johnny, rather than Mira and her unborn child. Only Adele Will could answer that, but where was she?

The case was close to falling in my lap. The loose ends, though, had yet to be tied up neatly. At this point, I wasn't sure what part Zac played in this.

How can the son, living in the same house, not know what his mother was up to? Another very serious angle I considered was this: that the unborn child was Zac's, and somehow Adele figured that Mira was fooling around with Zac and hence deserved to die.

Nope, the angle didn't have that kick.

My favourite man for the role of the cold-blooded murderer would always be Johnny, the one guy who had easy access to the morphine and the records. Question is, why would Johnny give morphine to his aunt, whom he detested?

Whichever way I saw it, one thing was certain – even if Adele had committed the murders, she could not have done it without help. There was more than one person involved. She may have an acid tongue and a brilliant scheming mind, but her body had deserted her. I drove fast towards the rehab. Summer had given way to winter and finally I was going to go home. Despite the rush, I felt a lightness of spirit that came with knowing that the task was near completion.

I found Zac on the phone with Anna, making plans for the evening. The look of amazement on Zac's face as I cut the line and took the receiver from his hand was priceless. He stood up, looking guilty as a murderer.

'What . . . are you doing?' he stammered.

'Where is your mother?'

'Out of town.'

'Very convenient for you.'

'I don't understand.'

'I found this in your dustbin.' I dangled the ampoule in front of him.

'What were you doing in my house?' Funny, how people worry about mundane things when so much is at stake.

'Zac, have you been supplying morphine to your mother?'

'Oh, for heaven's sake, what would mother need morphine for?'

He didn't know. He didn't know about her illness. Okay, I was going to be the harbinger of bad news then. I braced myself for the drama that would unfold.

'She has metastatic bone cancer.'

Zac was stunned for a moment and then he said to himself, 'She's dying.' He recovered quickly and asked, 'Why are you looking for my mother?'

'I think your mother killed Mira.'

'You are out of your mind . . . why would she kill Mira?'

'To hurt Johnny.'

'My mother is vindictive but she's not a murderer!'

'Oh, you'll be surprised; the things parents do for their children.'

'She did this for me? Now, you are talking absolute nonsense.'

'If Johnny goes to jail, you get the property as the next legal heir.'

'Really, then why not kill Johnny once and for all?'

'You tell me? You tried once. Your mother probably figured that Mira was a soft target and she could get away with it by framing Johnny.'

'My mother doesn't have that kind of ingenuity. She's just a shrill old woman. Leave her alone, she's had a tough life,' he said vehemently. The veins on his forehead were ready to burst.

'Well, the son-to-the-rescue act is touching, but I do need to see your mother.'

He spat at the floor and stomped out of the room. I had no

other option but to leave. Adele was the key to the whole thing. She was living on borrowed time. A stakeout outside her house was my best bet. She was bound to return home at some point tonight.

Sera

With Child

Thinking of the events of the nightmarish week, I pushed the bowl of soup aside and went back to the room. My appetite had deserted me and I didn't sleep too well. I had thrown up again this morning.

Johnny had watched me quietly from the door. I had to tell him. I was in Mira's shoes. I was pregnant and as lost as once she must have been.

I told him. He slapped me.

'It's yours, Johnny, I haven't been with anyone else in the last three years.'

Azaan's painting was fresh in our minds. How our closest betray us, I thought.

'Don't you pass on someone else's filth as mine!' he screamed.

I wish I was dead. Life, people, everything seemed ugly. I tried to convince him, pleading.

'The doctor told Adele I can never have children,' he said in a lost voice.

'Mira was engaged to you and she was with child too.'

'No, it's not true, Adele said I can't, I can't! You lying

bitch.' The forceful tone of his voice, the menacing look on his face made me step back in fear.

'Adele lied! She's the liar, not I.'

A stunned Johnny sat down on the floor. All the time repeating, 'Adele . . . Adele said the child wasn't mine. Adele won't lie.'

I tried to hug him; he pushed me away with such force that I lost my balance. And like always, he didn't come to save me from falling.

I fell yet again, fell hard. Johnny walked towards me, but did not give me a hand.

'Will you swear that this child is mine?'

'Yes, yes, Johnny, I swear this child is ours!'

With great difficulty, I pulled myself up. As soon as I got up, he began throwing the furniture. I had never seen such rage. He went berserk, stamping his foot, pulling the curtain, whimpering like a child and breaking everything in his way.

'She ruined my mother and now she's out to get me.'

'We'll be fine, Johnny.'

He looked at me strangely and said, 'You don't understand, do you? Mira is fucking dead . . . dead because of her!'

I was trained to handle such situations, but my nerve failed me. I was so scared for Johnny. He looked like he was having a breakdown.

'Calm down, Johnny, please I beg you. Adele is not important.'

'Oh, Sera! If you only knew what Adele has cost me!'

'Johnny, we'll figure all that out, here, drink some water.'

I handed him the glass fearing he might break it; he did, right at my feet. Blood trickled from his finger, where the shard had pierced his skin. I shuddered at the thought of what was to come. Suddenly, he became quiet. He stood there, still as a statue, for a whole minute before he spoke again.

'You know, I saw them, her and my father together, when I was five.'

I waited for him to speak. Five minutes passed, ten, then fifteen. At last, I mustered up the courage to shake him. He pulled me close and hugged me tight, like a child clinging to his mother.

'Zac and I were playing hide and seek and it was my turn to hide. They were in the basement. Her long black hair covered his face. I had never seen her hair out of a bun. She was beautiful and she laughed at something father said . . . or did.'

Silence again.

I kissed the top of his head to reassure him. He hugged me tight and said, 'I went straight to my mother and asked why papa didn't hug and kiss her like he did Aunt Adele. Nothing was ever the same again, Sera.'

The Face in the Window

Every word through the bathroom window fell clearly in my ears. This is a favourite place; from here, I used to spy on Robin and Daisy in my younger days. The brown face in the window is mine. Remembering a trembling Sera's scared reaction made me laugh.

Settle down more comfortably, Adele Will, there's a long night ahead of you. I had seen Officer Ray speaking to Zac. I believe the cat is out of the bag. I would have liked to spare Zac the anguish of finding out about me from another.

Sometimes, for greater good, one has to put loved ones through pain. His future was secure. No more working for the Johnnys of the world.

I could now die in peace.

My son would have everything that was rightfully his. The smart Johnny Will had signed more than half of his assets to the illegitimate younger brother. I could have insisted upon the house, but Thy Will has brought me nothing but misery. It was a prison, which Johnny and Johnny alone deserved.

I had lied to Johnny.

The doctor said that infertility was a likely long-term effect of the trauma. Going by the two pregnant women in Johnny's life, it never came to pass.

My greatest pleasure in life was to see Johnny suffer. 'Half a man' – a taunt he had lived with for so long. The poor boy would never believe the child was his.

I pitied Sera. Still, she is a lucky girl, alive, unlike Mira, who never got far enough to confide in Johnny. I had taken care of that. She had bumped into me at the clinic during my routine check-up. A few kind words and she was more than willing to share the news with Johnny's only other living family member.

She did not want the child. 'We are too young to take on the responsibility.'

I had felt like slapping the whore. I was twenty-two when I had Zac and I had taken good care of him, in spite of not having a penny to my name.

Yet another heir to Thy Will. I would have strangled her. But there are less painful ways to kill. Mira died without suffering, unlike the general.

In my old age, I realized that I had always been attracted to the underdog, the failures in life. The old drunk had imagined himself to be in love with me and could not bear to see the cancer eat away at my bones. He was pathetic, even when he was sober. I felt a kinship to him and looked forward to his routine evening visits and we chatted until it was time to shut the café.

Had the general not seen from his bedroom what he saw that day, life would have carried on all the same for everyone.

I had to kill him. It was easy, drunk and drugged; he hadn't posed any problem when I had led him to the kitchen garden.

Back in the old days, Robin and I used to get together to snatch a few after-dinner moments before he went and slept next to her . . .

I hate men.

The look in the general's eyes had been expectant. Men are so foolish, sixteen or sixty; they think women can't just get enough of them. Bastards.

The knife from Marie's kitchen came handy. It was such an outlet for my rage against this breed of men that my dying body felt resurrected. He couldn't scream, for the first blow had severed his neck from his body in one swift movement. There wasn't any need to persist, but I had stabbed him again and again. My work done, I waited patiently for Johnny to transfer the assets.

He went away for two weeks and on his return had a few surprises for me. He had papers transferring most of his assets in Zac's name and a new bride. The heat of the investigation too was beginning to settle, and it had looked like Johnny would get away scot-free. He nearly did.

Ah, the sweet taste of revenge! I no longer needed the morphine to suppress the pain that gnawed at my bones. The balm of revenge is far more soothing.

The story that had begun at twenty-two with Robin was going to end with his son paying for his misdeed. Robin's fear had mercilessly ruined any chance that he, Zac and I might have had of being a proper family. His son deserved no better, I have seen to that. No man can live with the guilt of killing his unborn child. He'll breathe in free air, but he'll never be truly free. Just like Robin, his guilt would kill him, painfully, slowly.

I remember vividly the look on Johnny's face when I had

shared Mira's good news with him. How the woman in his life was with another man's child.

I had seen blood in Johnny's eyes. Next morning, Mira was found dead. All this seems such a long time ago.

Well, Sera is pregnant and Johnny's punishment is about to begin.

Scent of a Killer

We found Adele's body outside the bathroom window in the morning. I am told by Marie that, twenty years ago, Daisy was found dead in a similar manner on the other side of that window. History has a way of repeating itself. She had died some time during the night. I knelt on the ground to collect the torn pages from the general's journal that were scattered around her. Well, they weren't of much use now, neither the poetry, nor the bit about Johnny being in Mira's apartment. All was rendered null and void by a single piece of paper Adele clutched in her skinny hands.

The note was written with shaking hands, as one would write in a moving train. Sentences ran across paper, twirled and collapsed, with the last breath that had left her body. The words were painted in the blood that she had coughed all over the note and herself.

> *I, Adele Will, hereby confess to having killed Mira Kermani. I could not bear the thought of another heir to Thy Will. I hope to make Johnny pay for all the atrocities he has committed against me and my son by throwing us out of Thy Will.*

I stole a box of morphine from the rehab, drugged Mira and left her for dead.

I killed the general too, he saw me in Mira's apartment from his bedroom. I buried him in the kitchen garden. A drunk is like a lamb to sacrifice if one knows how to use a butcher's knife. The poor fellow was in love with me. Perhaps no one told him that love kills.

My sincere apology to my son Zac. I have been a bad mother. I promise to do better in the next lifetime. I love you, Zac, and so did your father. Forgive me.

Adele

Everyone heaved a sigh of relief at finding the note, Kermani, Sera, Marie, Johnny, even Zac. At last, they knew it was an old bitter woman, who had acted upon her hate. It didn't make things better or bring back the dead, but it made sense and that's all these people wanted – to make sense out of things, to find closure. To me, however, the case was far from closed, for there was an odd discrepancy in Adele's note. She had written in her letter, 'I stole a box of morphine from the rehab.' 'A box' meant one box; then who took the other box? One box was still unaccounted for. The ampoule that I found in her dustbin came from a different box.

If Adele was the killer, she would have known that the dosage used to kill Mira was 200 mg, which meant that the entire contents of one box had been emptied into Mira's blood stream. Yet, Adele had a surplus of morphine, which she was using to ease her pain. Where did that box come from? Why did she need it? I have no way of proving this, but in my opinion, the box was given to Adele and not stolen by her.

Was she covering up? But covering up for whom?

It couldn't be for Zac. Zac was the one to report the missing boxes. That left only Sera and Johnny. Adele hated Johnny, and Sera was no dearer to her.

Why would Adele lie on her deathbed, unless she had struck a deal with the devil himself?

Darling Adele

Summer is here. And so is the baby. I have named her Dee, after Daisy and Adele. She smiles as I pick her up and we stroll in the garden. Dee's birth has brought Sera and me close. Our combined energy is now focused on raising her right. These moments of peace are few and far between. I often wake up in the middle of the night to find Mira sitting by my bedside. Sometimes Robin and Adele like to visit too. I am sane enough to realize that they are in my dreams, but ask anyone how real the horrors of a nightmare are. My reality is no different; it is coloured with the lies of the past and the present.

For seventeen years, Adele lost no opportunity to drill into me that I was half a man. How could I believe the baby was mine? I can't claim that I didn't know what I was doing. I went to Mira's house prepared to end her lies, our relationship.

That very afternoon, Adele had flashed her cancer report along with Mira's pregnancy report. Her tut-tutting had me enraged, but she calmed me down saying, 'I got very little time to live, Johnny, don't be angry with me now. I just showed you the report so that you know the whore you are bedding.'

'Get out, Adele, before I do something we both will regret.'

'Now, don't be rude, Johnny. I only came to ask for morphine. They refused to give it to me at the clinic. The pain's killing me! I can't even get out of bed in the morning to make Zac breakfast with these fucking cramps. Will you take that away from a son – the last few meals his mother can make him?' She had stood there, smiling, daring me to refuse.

'And darling, don't tell Zac . . . about the cancer or the morphine.'

I sent her home, saying I will bring it over in the evening. How was I to know that evening was going to be one hell of a black evening.

Mira wasn't home when I knocked on her door. I waited in my car. She returned shortly after I had begun to draw her sketch. I waited five minutes and pressed the buzzer to her apartment. She opened the door in a white silk dress. White was my favourite colour, but that evening it seemed revolting to me. I had walked in, indifferent to her chatter, to her arms around my neck.

She pressed a glass of wine in my hand and stood there playing with the stem of her wine glass. When she started speaking, all that poured from her mouth were lies, about how I was going to be the father of her child. I had seen the note on the orchids Azaan had sent her. It was Azaan's seed in her womb.

Yet, she kept insisting it was mine. I wouldn't have used the morphine that night, but she kept saying that the baby was mine. She was sobbing and hurling abuses at me for not believing her. It reminded me of a scene from my parents' bedroom, fighting and crying, the daily drama. In that moment, I just wanted her to shut the fuck up. I took out the morphine that was meant for Adele, to calm Mira down. I don't know how it happened, or why I snapped. It's all very hazy; I remember injecting her till she stopped screaming . . . breathing.

I held her close, watched her die as I had watched my father die years ago, as the spark from his cigarette burnt a hole in the carpet and soon it all caught fire.

I watched from the window as he tried to douse the flames from his clothes, his skin. Robin could have been saved but I ignored his pleas for help and sat down to add the finishing touches to Zac's sketch.

I didn't understand why he was screaming for help; this was the release father had been hankering after, drowning his soul in alcohol. When he finally stopped kicking and screaming, I called for help. They declared him dead. I felt nothing, except relief at being free. No more drinking, shouting and name-calling. I was relieved that my father was dead. There was not a hint of guilt or remorse. I was happy for myself and for Zac and Marie, and that's the truth.

It's twisted, warped; as a psychiatrist I understand it has deeper ramifications. Somewhere, my psyche was deeply splintered, the result of which led me to murder a woman I once loved.

In my hurry to get away from Mira, I forgot to take the sketch and it fell into Officer Ray's capable hands. Strange are the ways of destiny. Ray was once again at my throat. By the time I reached Thy Will, the enormity of my mistake had settled in. Adele was there waiting for me in my study to spring a few surprises of her own. She walked up to the window and pulled the curtain aside. The general was standing there taking a swig from his flask, clutching at a sheaf of papers. She offered to help.

'You are in big trouble, Johnny. He saw what you did. He came running to tell me, how my nephew was injecting his girlfriend with drugs. What did you do to her, Johnny?'

'She will be fine . . . in the morning.'

'Will she?'

She picked up the empty syringe from my desk and said, 'What did you do, Johnny? You have that look on your face . . .'

'She's dead, Adele.'

That took the wind out of her sails. She sat down with a thud. 'Oh, Johnny, what have you done? Johnny! What have you done?'

'I thought you would be happy, Adele. Isn't this what you wanted, Thy Will, all to yourself?'

'No, no, it's all my fault . . . I can't, I won't let you go to jail. Your father will never forgive me.'

'Stop it, Adele, don't talk as if he's alive! Get out of here. I don't want your help. No one is going to believe the ravings of a drunk anyway.'

'He has a journal, Johnny. He notes everything in it, just like you said he should. I have read it. It doesn't read like the ramblings of a madman. He can put you away for a long time. Do you want to be locked up?'

'No.'

'I can fix it, Johnny. Trust me, I will take care of you. Your father would want me to.'

I was scared; I had no one to turn to. She was the only family I knew and I leant on her. It was a mistake.

Adele proposed that I sign half the assets to Zac's name and she would make sure that the general would never tell a single soul about what had transpired in Mira's apartment. She said, the stupid fool imagined himself to be in love with her and she knew how to keep him quiet.

There wasn't much of a choice. I knew the general wouldn't pass up an opportunity to screw me over after the way I had treated him.

I told Adele the paperwork of transferring assets in Zac's name would take a week. She promised to keep her end of the bargain – keeping the general quiet.

I had no idea at that time that she was willing to go to any lengths to keep him silent. Adele knew very well she couldn't keep a drunk from talking. She butchered the general the same night and hid the body in my backyard to buy time. Adele used to go hunting with Grandpa Will. She was good with a knife. Unlike other girls her age, she could skin a chicken alive. Grandpa Will always said Adele should have been a boy.

On her way out of my study, she picked up the syringe. There was some morphine remaining and she injected the general with it. Hacking the head of an unconscious man was child's play for Adele.

She dumped the syringe along with the body under the pile of compost. All Adele needed was a week's time to make Zac a wealthy man. No one was more shocked than me when the general's body was discovered in my backyard, in the very garden my mother used to grow vegetables. Adele screwed me over again. She watched me squirm from a distance, as I lied to the police and to Sera, and struggled to stay sane.

But in the end, Adele made good on her promise of taking care of me, by confessing to my crime. Her confession cleared my name, along with any doubt people had about my involvement in Mira's death – all except one: Officer Ray. He was smart enough to pick up the discrepancy in the note about one box of morphine.

He came around sniffing, convinced that someday he would find something against me and drag me out of Thy Will. Without any proof, his empty threats had no meaning. As always, I out stared him and he promised to return.

In truth, I don't care anymore. What really bothered me was Adele's behaviour. She could have died peacefully, even got some respect, something she never got when she was alive. Yet, she chose to die as painfully and horribly as she had lived for thirty-five long years. Even in her death, she would be remembered as a vindictive woman.

Yet, a vengeful person like Adele is not supposed to or expected to confess to a murder, to save the nephew she hated; a question that keeps me awake many nights. Why did she do it? The only answer that comes to me is that sometimes when people love, they love deeply. Sometimes ordinary, selfish, vengeful people display extraordinary love and courage in the face of hurt, anger and disappointment. She must have truly loved my father.

I also think of him often. It must have been awfully lonely for him; one wrong turn, wrong choice, had led him down a lonely road. I remember his bony hands clutching at my shoulders when I struggled to lift him up as he lay drunk on the floor. He weighed a mere fifty-seven kilos at the time of his death.

He had sobbed on my shoulder, while the wind blew

wisps of hair from his balding head. 'Johnny, help me, I want to stop. I don't know how to stop.'

'Just stop drinking, Papa. Throw the bottle away!'

'I try, I can't . . . it feels like I am going to die if I don't drink. I can't bear the pain.'

'Then die, before you kill us all.'

His frailty no longer affected me like it did when as a child I would go running to lift him up. 'Papa, Papa, wake up! Papa, get up.' I had only felt disgust at the weakness of that man who, day after day, drank, blabbered, cursed and passed out in his drunken stupor. Disgusted, I left him sobbing on the floor, asking for my help. I could hear his cries all the way to my room, but I didn't pick him up. In the morning, I found him soaked and sleeping in his own urine. He had not managed to crawl to the bathroom. I wasn't proud of myself in the morning, but at least I didn't go running like my mother did every time he yelped.

Perhaps that's where I went wrong; had I helped him that night and the nights after that, maybe I would have turned out to be a different man. I have come to the conclusion that when we refuse to help another, our heart begins to harden, and we lose our humanity. Not lifting him up was my biggest mistake; that was the moment I lost my humanity.

I lost it to the resentment and hatred I carried in my heart for my father and his lifestyle. If he was weak, I was weaker. He needed help, not harsh words of admonishment and rebuke. Never before did I realize how lonely he was, all alone in the prison of his mind; now I do, as I rot in mine.

I rocked my chair as I sat cross-legged on the porch, watching my wife and my child. I was tapping the floor with my foot. Lately, I had been doing it often; it was a sign of nervous energy. Marie scolded me, saying that I had picked this annoying habit from my father. He'd drum his foot as he waited for morning to become noon, a respectable hour around which he could pull out the bottle and load up the icebox. I was well on my way to becoming my father's son.

The orange ball of fire was setting across the mountains, signalling night would be here soon. Dee was in her pram, throwing up her hands, laughing as babies do, without a care in the world. Sera cooed to her, while she watered the roses in full bloom. Motherhood suited her; it gave her radiance, a certain glow that came from being responsible for another life. To Sera, life couldn't be more perfect.

Poor, naïve Sera suspected nothing. She believed that my aunt's lies and betrayal were responsible for the hours I spent brooding, distancing myself from her. She tried her best to draw me out, to engage me. There were days I felt overwhelmed by her love, but in the end, the demons in my head always won.

I, who prided myself for being better than my spineless father, faint-hearted mother, underdog half-brother and deceitful aunt, how cold-bloodedly I had killed the woman I loved. I was the worst of them all, a hypocrite and a fraud. I now wish I had confessed to my crime and not let Adele 'fix things' for me.

Even in death, Adele had plans for me – a lifelong prison of her making.

Epilogue

Lari hobbles around the house, cooking and cleaning as before, but there's a strange tenderness in her eyes every time she gazes at her Johnny. She sees in him the same dejection and loneliness she saw in Robin's eyes. She suspects he may not have been innocent of Mira's death.

Razaan has gone back to London to paint, even though Uncle Kermani threatened to cut him off. He can't bear to be in a place where the murderer of Mira roams scotfree. He and Officer Ray have come to an agreement that someday Johnny will crack, and when he does, they'll be there to catch him, put him behind bars.

Sera is happy enough with the baby and happier still that Johnny has agreed to psychotherapy. She finds him withdrawn and distant, but not even for a moment does she doubt his love for her. She can't help but marvel at her good fortune to have married a man who is a philanthropist at heart. She quite by chance discovered that, for years now, a large portion of what Johnny makes at Thy Will is pumped into Alcoholic Anonymous around the country. To Sera, there is no finer man than Johnny in the world.

is even more grateful than before to Johnny for his generosity in signing over half the estate in his name. His loyalty to Johnny is unquestionable. Zac has also bought a new house, but he misses Adele terribly. It isn't as neat and clean as it used to be when his mother was around. He is considering marrying Anna, a control freak and a manipulative woman, but it's the closest he feels to being at home.

has sent many a written request to the police commissioner seeking permission to continue working on the Kermani case. He has been told categorically that the case is closed. Officer Ray believes that, proof or no proof, the real killer is Johnny Will.

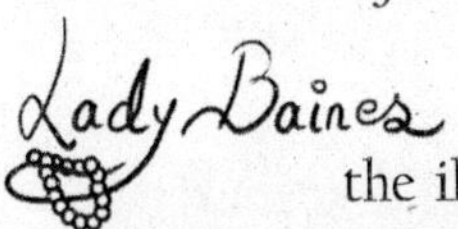

is at peace, counselling the locals about the ill effects of alcohol. She's converted her home into a centre for women and families who need guidance and support to deal with an alcoholic family member.

has left the running of Seven Seas to the board and has gone back to Bombay, from where he had come twenty years ago with his wife and his little daughter.

wears a perpetually pained expression. People call it mourning; Johnny knows it to be guilt.